Finn

Hathaway House, Book 6

Dale Mayer

Books in This Series:

FINN: HATHAWAY HOUSE, BOOK 6
Dale Mayer
Valley Publishing Ltd.

ISBN-13: 978-1-773362-77-9
Print Edition

About This Book

Welcome to Hathaway House, a heartwarming and SWEET military romance series from USA TODAY best-selling author Dale Mayer. Here you'll meet a whole new group of friends, along with a few favorite characters from Heroes for Hire. Instead of action, you'll find emotion. Instead of suspense, you'll find healing. Instead of romance, ... oh, wait. ... There is romance—of course!

Welcome to Hathaway House. Rehab Center. Safe Haven. Second chance at life and love.

Navy SEAL Finn MacGregor arrives at Hathaway House not only with half of one leg but with a stoma, one that necessitates the use of a colostomy bag. While it's nice to once again see his old friend Dani Hathaway and her father, the Major, it's tough to feel like the least sexy man on the face of the earth. Especially after he meets the pretty nurse in charge of his care ...

Fiona Smithers has seen practically everything when it comes to the human body, and Finn's physical problems don't faze her. Emotionally she's wary though. Once before, one of her patients had confused the gratitude he felt for her as love. ... That scenario left Fiona devastated to know her friendliness had been misunderstood. Whether deemed love or friendliness, those emotions directly effected that patient's initial healing and then his setbacks of body as well as of heart and of mind, making her more determined not to run the same risks again.

Yet, this time, she may not be able to help herself. She wants Finn in her life on a permanent basis, but, after seeing his obsession with her in his artwork, is that even possible?

Sign up to be notified of all Dale's releases here!
https://smarturl.it/DaleNews

Prologue

SURELY HATHAWAY HOUSE couldn't be that good. Finn MacGregor couldn't believe the emails he'd received from Elliot about the success of his healing therapies … and about Sicily.

They had to be fiction. Elliot didn't have a girlfriend already? And not just a girlfriend but like a wedding in the near future?

How could that be?

Finn knew that a lot of good women would take on a man less than whole, but Elliot sounded like a completely different person. Originally Finn had tossed off Elliot's interest in Sicily as infatuation, but now, months down the road, apparently not. Finn had told Elliot about applying for a transfer, but Finn's multiple surgeries had pushed that back.

And rightly so, but, as Finn lay in bed, worn out and so done with doctors and this hospital, he realized that maybe now was the right time.

He was at a crossroads. This was the end of his surgeries, and now it was all about making the best of who and what he was today.

No need to transfer to another center to get that, but he wanted a change of faces, smells and scenery. And Hathaway House sounded divine. He'd been raised on a ranch in

Texas. That alone made him want to go. Any chance to go home—particularly at this stage of his life—was good.

A text came in. He lifted his phone and checked the message. It was from Elliot.

Put in your request. They have beds opening up and a cancellation. No better time than right now.

This was the right time for a lot of reasons. But instead of filling out the request form, he dialed a number he'd looked at many times.

When a woman answered, he said, "Dani? It's Finn. Any chance you've got a bed there?"

"For you, I'll find one. How soon can you come?"

"As soon as you can make it happen," he said, a silly grin on his face. It would be good to see her again. He'd met her years ago when he was with his friends Levi and Stone. They'd kept in touch, but only through Elliot had Finn realized who ran the center.

Lord, it would be good to go home.

Chapter 1

F INN MACGREGOR, WITH the help of the aide behind him, slowly pushed his way up the ramp in his wheelchair. He could see that, over time, this ramp would be a lot easier, just like so many other ramps in his life. Being in a wheelchair sucked. He'd had high hopes of getting out of it at the beginning, and that hope had faded over time. But now that he was at Hathaway House, his friend Dani's place, with Elliot, another friend, here to cheer him on, Finn had reinvested into that same hope again.

He knew it was a bit foolish, but, when a man was down and out, hope was one of the biggest things that kept him going.

The aide pushed a little harder behind Finn. When they reached the top of the gradual slope, Finn twisted and looked up at the big man behind him, smiled and said, "Thanks."

His voice cheerful, as if he'd done this many times before, the man replied, "No problem. Next time you can do it all on your own. You did pretty well getting here as it is."

The name tag on the man's shirt read Malcolm. "Well, Malcolm, hopefully it won't take too long to make that kind of progress."

"It won't," Malcolm said. "All kinds of miracles happen here."

Finn straightened up as the huge double doors opened,

letting Malcolm push him into the front reception area. Finn stopped and stared at the massive open space and all the long hallways that conjoined right at the reception area. An office was off to the side, light music played and absolutely nothing was institutional about this place. More like the lounge of a bed-and-breakfast.

Finn frowned. "Are you sure this is the right place?" he joked.

Malcolm, a big yet quiet smile on his face, nodded and said, "Not only is it the right place but that person has been waiting for you." He pointed to a woman walking quickly toward Finn.

He stared at her and felt a shock of recognition. "Dani?"

She let out a peal of laughter, opened her arms wide, bent down and gave him a big hug.

He wrapped his arms around her as best he could. Just feeling her arms tighten around him made his eyes leak a bit. "Damn," he said, "I should have tried to get here earlier."

"I told you to," she said, "but I must wait until people are ready. Ready to make that kind of move. It's not easy to do, and I'm really proud of you for having made it."

Again he felt that light prick of pride inside. He had to remind himself that pride went before the fall, and he'd already had enough falls in his life. He glanced around and said, "Honestly, I thought Elliot was off his rocker with everything he's been telling me about your place here, and I'm so proud of you for having done what you've done. This place is huge."

"It is, indeed," she said, "and getting bigger every day. We are adding a wing up and down. Here for the humans and downstairs for the animals' vet."

Finn nodded. Elliot had filled him in on how this rehab

center catered to both injured animals and humans. They had a massive veterans clinic and rehab center here, where veterans came home with more than a few health issues, had gone through surgeries, and now needed specialized care to get them back on their feet. This wasn't a long-term facility for people who had no improvements to be made. This was a place where people came to get their strength back and to learn how to become mobile with whatever body parts they had replaced—or, in some cases, didn't have replaced.

Finn stared at his missing lower leg and frowned.

"Not to worry about your leg," Dani said, her gaze following his. "You're just one of many here."

He winced at that. "Somehow that's not reassuring."

"It will be," she said. She walked behind the reception area, picked up a file and then said, "Come on. Let's get you to your room. The sooner we get you settled, the sooner we can start having fun."

As they headed down the hall, he asked her, "How long have you guys been open now?"

"Seven years," she replied. "But, of course, getting the word out is a whole different story. This last year has been incredible though," she admitted.

"Sounds like it's well-deserved with the kind of success Elliot has been spouting off about. If it's even one-tenth as good as what he's been telling me," he said, "it's got to be fantastic."

"We've had a lot of really good successes," Dani said with a bright smile. "But with all that comes one case which just gives you no end of trouble. And we've had a couple people who have come here and then decided it was not for them and left."

"I think that goes for everything in life," Finn said. "We

are not all geared for the same things."

She turned to Malcolm and said, "We're heading for 212."

Malcolm nodded. They took the next corner, went down a short hall and turned Finn's wheelchair to face the door with big black numbers proclaiming 212.

Dani opened the door, and Malcolm pushed Finn through the extra-wide doorway. The room was large. Had his own private bathroom. There was a dresser and a large double bed with all the equipment that went with his disabilities. He stared at all the hooks and chains and winced. "I sure hope I don't ever need those," he said, motioning at the apparatus above the bed.

She walked over, and, with the push of a button, the apparatus retracted against the wall. "I'd be happy to never have to touch that again for you," she said cheerfully. "But it's there if you need it. Physiotherapy specialists and doctors will decide how much of that you might need."

He nodded, staring up at it. "Very high-tech," he murmured.

"We try," she said. "Do you want to get into bed right now?"

He hesitated.

"Otherwise, we can go over the paperwork. I'll give you your iPad and then I can take you for a tour, and we can sit out on the deck with a cup of coffee."

He brightened at that. "That sounds much more informal and more my style."

She grinned. "Here's your iPad with your schedule and more information, if you're curious. I want you to flick through it all. Your team has been assigned to you, and they are all available for messaging on that tablet, custom designed for us. You'll see all the names of everybody who will be working with you. I'll leave this paperwork here. You can take a look at it when we get back and you're on your own. Obviously, you have some personal effects coming."

Malcolm stood by the doorway and said, "I'll grab his stuff at reception."

Dani smiled up at him. "Thanks, Malcolm."

She turned toward Finn. "When we get back after coffee, you can put your stuff away, so that it feels more like home. Let's head down, and I'll show you around."

As they wheeled out with her pushing him, he said, "I can wheel myself, you know?"

"Good," she said, "but sometimes it's nice to be wheeled around. You're tired and stressed with your travels, and I need to make sure that your stress levels are minimized. So how about letting your old friend push you around?"

He sagged into the wheelchair, his back easing because, of course, it *did* hurt his back to do the wheeling. It was one of the things that his prior doctors had not been happy about. He was missing a big swath of muscle along one side, not to mention the kidney on the right side, and of course, the shrapnel had eaten away part of the muscles around it. After the act of removing that shrapnel, they had put as much of Finn back together as possible. Multiple surgeries later, he was as good as he would get, but he was weak on one side. That was his job to fix now.

She whispered, "Good way to start."

He chuckled. "We go way back, kiddo. I can't believe we're at this stage of our lives."

"Not sure about you," she said, "but I'm engaged to be married. Remember Dad? He's here too."

"The major?" Finn asked with a laugh. "Man, back then

I wasn't so sure he would make it."

"Neither was I," Dani said, all her laughter falling away. "He started this center, I think, more as a project to help himself and to help his buddies, but since then he's a completely different person. We'd have been lost without this center all these years."

Finn watched as they headed down the short hallway and into the main hallway, and almost immediately she turned a corner, and there it opened up a huge section, the entrance to a large eating area. He stared to see tables and chairs and couches, more like little community sitting areas.

"We redid part of this area so that it was a more of a sitting room," she said. "Pretty happy with the way it worked out." She carried on, pushing him forward into what opened up to a massive cafeteria.

He stared in surprise. "Wow. I was expecting little trays on hospital trolleys."

"That can be arranged too," she said. "If you need a meal in your room, then don't hesitate to ask. When you've had enough of the people or the physical work, or you're just too damn tired, or you're just too depressed, and you don't want to make the effort to come in for a meal, we'd all appreciate it if you would at least call for a meal so that somebody can come and check up on you and bring you something hot to eat."

"I'll remember that," he said in surprise.

"We're much more of a family here," she said. "You'll get to know the characters around the place fairly quickly."

"Looks like it." He watched several people at the cafeteria counter pushing trays in front of them, some with legs, some on crutches, some in wheelchairs.

She pushed him into the line, pulled a tray down and

placed it beside him as they moved along. "Are you hungry?" she asked.

He flushed and shook his head. "No. Just coffee will be fine."

"Right," she said. "I forgot, but I have to add a couple notes on that for your PT to consider."

"What notes?" he asked gruffly.

"Notes about your system," she said. "Not that you have allergies but you have a lot of food sensitivities."

He shrugged. What he was sensitive to was the way his food had to travel. Who knew that he would lose most of his bowels and need a colostomy bag? How embarrassing was that? He'd heard lots of other people say it made no bloody difference, but Finn had yet to come to that point. Who liked to poop out of their side? That was just gross. And every time he ate food, it reminded him that it had to go in one way and come out another.

Almost as if she understood what he was thinking about, she bent and said, "I guess you don't want a bran muffin with too much fiber then, do you?"

He glared at her. She smiled, a secretive smile, as if she knew something he didn't.

She pushed him up to the coffee station. There, she poured two cups and said, "If you don't want anything to eat, I'll grab a muffin." She placed it on the tray with butter and a knife and then looked around and said, "Where would you like to sit? Inside or out?" She pointed to a whole wall that opened up to an outdoor section of the cafeteria.

"Outdoors," he said instantly.

She placed the tray in his lap and said, "You get to look after that."

She wheeled him past several other groups of men out in

the sunshine. As Finn studied the inside area, he thought he caught a glimpse of a dog. Maybe a therapy dog? As they shifted into the hot sun, he tilted his head back and smiled. There was something absolutely glorious about having the sun on his face.

She removed the tray to place it on the table before pushing him up close and taking a seat across from him. He didn't even want to face her; he was enjoying the morning sunshine so much.

"There's something just so wrong about being in an institution for so long," she murmured. "Getting out in the sun and feeling it deep in your soul is so very healing." Just then she called out, "Elliot!"

Instantly Finn's eyes opened. He twisted to see her pointing at somebody. He twisted around a little more, almost crying out, barely stifling the gasp of pain as he took the motion too far and settled back, gasping at first, then trying to breathe deeply to ease the pain. She waited calmly at his side. When he could, he said, "Sorry, that was foolish of me."

"Limitations of the body are not something any of us ever like to admit," she said calmly.

"I guess you're used to it, aren't you?"

"Nobody ever gets used to somebody's pain," she said with the gentlest of smiles that he remembered so well.

She had always been all heart, this girl.

"And living in a place where every person lives with pain helps me to realize how grateful I am to be pain-free."

"Good point," he said. He shifted in the wheelchair to ease the pain in his back when he felt a hand clap on his shoulder. He looked up to see Elliot Carver, an old friend, standing above him. Finn reached up to shake his hand, but

Elliot bent and hugged him hard.

"Damn, I'm glad to see you finally here," he said with a big smile. He looked at Dani and back over at Finn. "Do you mind if I grab a chair and sit down?"

"Hell no," he said. "Please, join us."

Elliot grabbed a chair and dropped into it at Finn's side.

Just the ease of Elliot's movement and how comfortable he was in his own body now struck Finn as odd. Not so much odd, just ... so natural and so graceful. It made Finn realize how awkward he was in his own physical state. He was unappreciative of his body, and, in some ways, it felt as if he'd been paired up with a brand-new partner in the military and they hadn't had time to work out their idiosyncrasies to blend together. It had never been like that before. He'd always been a perfectly fit physical specimen.

Until the accident.

And now, well, now it was as if he hated his body and his body hated him.

"You look absolutely fantastic," Finn said to Elliot.

Elliot grinned. "Well, besides the fact that I'm healing at an incredibly fast rate—and Dani here would say that emotional and physical and mental healing also has to happen in order for us to move forward in leaps and bounds," he said, "I am happy. I'm fit. I feel good, and, for the first time in a long time, it feels as if life isn't like I pulled the short straw."

Finn immediately recognized the feeling. "Right," he said, "and I'm still stuck not only with the short straw but it's way shorter than it was originally."

Elliot burst out laughing at that. "Oh, I do remember feeling that too," he said. "There's only so much in life that we can really blame others for before we have to deal with the reality of what we're stuck with." He motioned at the missing lower leg on Finn's right stump and asked, "Have you been fitted for prosthetics yet?"

"They had to do more surgery to change the way the stump was because the prosthetics were soring me up," he said, "I haven't had a chance to try again. I'm hoping to do that while I'm here." He glanced at Dani with one eyebrow raised.

Dani immediately nodded. "That'll be one of the first things we try to get you into, but, in the meantime, you'll have crutches."

He winced at that. "The back and the right shoulder don't like crutches," he said apologetically.

She gave him a serene smile that immediately made him suspicious.

Finn glanced at Elliot, who was also grinning. "I'll get crutches and will have to suffer through it, won't I?" he asked glumly.

"You will," Elliot said. "Hathaway House doesn't do too much on the babysitting level here, and you'll be glad for it. It's a tough journey to start. Yet it's an absolutely wonderful journey when you get to your destination."

"How much longer are you here for?" Finn asked, already worried. "I hope you're not leaving too quickly because it's partly because of you that I'm here," he said, glancing between Dani and Elliot.

"I'm here for one or two more months, but I think I get to graduate soon," Elliot said. "Just some fine-tuning now."

Immediately Finn felt lost, knowing he would be here much longer. He still had Dani, whom he knew, but Elliot had been somebody who knew him in his old life, understood what he'd gone through and understood what shit he was dealing with now. "Well, obviously I wish you all the best," he said lightly.

"No sending me away yet," Elliot said. "I'm still here for a while. Don't you worry. Besides, I'm likely to settle close to town."

At that, Finn frowned. "Why? Your family is back West, aren't they?"

"Not exactly sure where I'll end up yet," he said, "because I have some new family that really matters to me. So I'm not ready to pull up roots from here and go back there again."

"Just make sure it isn't an attachment to the recovery process," Finn warned.

Elliot laughed and laughed. "Oh my, I'm so glad you said that. Because you really need to have that mindset when it comes to dealing with the stuff you're going through here," he said as he turned to look at Dani. Elliot smiled. "Isn't that right, Dani?"

Dani smiled and nodded. She picked up half of her muffin and offered it to Finn.

He stared at it, his stomach grumbling. "But it's bran," he said. And then he winced. "You have no idea what bran does to an already damaged digestive system."

"Sometimes it's supposed to be the best thing," Dani said with a shrug. "But we have many other options, from carrot to chocolate chip."

At the words *chocolate chip*, his eyes lit up.

Elliot chuckled. "I'll go get myself one. Do you want one?"

Finn nodded slowly. "Well, I have to eat sometime," he said.

Dani agreed. "We have lots of other food choices here, if

you want something other than a muffin."

He remembered seeing all kinds of hot dishes inside, and he realized that, with the stress of moving, he had hardly eaten breakfast. Besides, the hospital food had been pallid, lukewarm and tasted like flat Jell-O. "Maybe," he said.

Elliot smiled and said, "How about I pick you out something? Do you promise to try it?"

Finn nodded. "Maybe not breakfast this time. A sandwich maybe? Nothing fancy," he said. "I'm not super hungry."

"I'll be back in a minute."

Finn watched as Elliot casually walked through the dining room as if he owned the world. "It's hard to believe the condition he's in," Finn said.

"True enough," Dani said. "All kinds of improvements are being made on many levels with every patient here. Don't judge anybody else or yourself. The scale doesn't slide evenly, and it doesn't slide in only one direction." At that, she stood and waved at somebody else. She leaned over and said, "Excuse me. I have to speak to somebody," and she disappeared around his back.

He sat here for a long moment, thinking about her words, acknowledging just how much truth was behind them. It had been the same in his recovery. Six SEALs had been in Finn's original team. Two had died during the mission—one more had taken his own life—and, of the three left, he would have considered himself to have been hurt the worst and showing the least amount of progress.

But he doubted the others would agree with him.

FIONA SMITHERS PICKED up two coffees and walked over to join the nurses at their favorite table before Fiona started her morning shift. She sat down to see Dani waving at her. She stood again, murmuring to the group, "Sorry. I need to talk to Dani." She walked across the cafeteria, holding a coffee in her hand, as Dani met her halfway.

"Hey, glad to have you back again," Dani said. "I forgot you were due in today."

Fiona chuckled. "How could you possibly have forgotten? Like I could leave this place for very long," she said affectionately. She gave Dani an awkward one-armed hug, making sure not to spill any coffee on her.

Of course, she'd come close to leaving a little while ago after a patient had perceived a personal relationship that wasn't there. The scenario had an ugly end, and she was still smarting from it. But life moved on, and the patient had left—thankfully—and the ensuing weeks had been calm and peaceful.

"I wanted to introduce you to my friend and a new resident here," Dani said.

"Only you would call them *residents*," Fiona said. "Nobody wants to live here. You know that, right?"

"Well, I'm a resident, and I live here," Dani said, chuckling, walking slowly to give Fiona some background on Finn. "His name is Finn. I knew him back in the first year after high school," Dani said. "We were volunteers for several animal organizations and used to do the Walk for Paws things to raise money. He went into the military at the end of that year, but we've bonded quite well during that time. When he needed a place for rehab, I offered it to him, but he wasn't ready. Finally, he gave me a quick call a couple days ago when we happened to have an empty bed, and I brought him in."

"Sounds like it was perfect timing," Fiona said. She wondered at the wisdom of bringing in friends to a place like this, but, so far, Dani had been very good about keeping personal relationships and paying clients on a very good balance. "Is he a good, *good* friend?"

Dani slid her a look and then chuckled. "He's a good friend but only a friend."

"I'm sure Aaron's relieved to hear that," Fiona said with a smirk.

Dani flushed. "Aaron trusts me, and I trust him," she said with a big smile. "We can't wait to get married."

"Good," Fiona said. "And that should be pretty darn soon, shouldn't it?"

"Potentially. We haven't really set a date and don't want to make too big a deal out of it. We might just get married in town and call it done," Dani said. "Life is busy, and I can't really have a wedding at home with everybody here. That's more than I want to put on people, so I might just do something small in town."

"Invite me when you do," Fiona said. "If I'm not working, I'd love to come."

Dani gave her a smile. "Will do," she said. "That's another issue. Whoever we invite will have to get others to cover their shifts, and I don't want hard feelings. So it's back to that whole 'might just do a few people in town' thing."

"Makes sense. We can always have a big reception afterward here. I'm sure the kitchen staff would be happy to put on something to celebrate the day, like we do for any other big holiday."

"You know what? That's not a bad idea," Dani said thoughtfully. "Aaron is coming home at Christmas time and

Thanksgiving."

"How's he doing in school?"

"I think it's rougher than he thought it would be," Dani said comfortably. "But it's his passion, and he's getting phenomenal grades. I think it's the toll of the daily studying and the exams and reports," she said with a smile. "And, of course, he wants to come home."

"Right," Fiona said. "I tried a long-distance relationship when I was in nursing school, but it wasn't for me."

"It's not for everyone," Dani said. "When you think about it, it's hard to be separated from the one you love." She approached the table where Finn sat and motioned at him.

Fiona looked at him and saw a shock of red hair that made her grin. Tall, lean, with freckles across his face that made him younger looking than he was, because she could see the world-weariness in his eyes, and the pain in his body as he held himself stiffly on one side. She recognized some of the aftermath of his injuries but was interested to hear what else was going on.

As Dani came around the table, she smiled at Finn. "Here's somebody I want you to meet. This is Fiona Smithers," she said, "one of our nurses here. You'll see her a fair bit. She's assigned to your team too."

Finn held out a hand, and Fiona shook it gently.

"Hi, nice to meet you," she said.

"Wow, somebody from the Old Country," Finn said.

"Maybe originally," Fiona said, "but it was generations ago."

"Well, I was born here too," Finn said, "but my mother's from Ireland."

That helped break the ice a little bit. He seemed to relax,

but she noted the pain up and down his spine just from the way he was trying to settle in his wheelchair. She glanced back at Dani. "Has he had all the intros to the place yet?"

"No," Dani said, "we got sidetracked here with coffee. Elliot's bringing him a sandwich."

Fiona nodded and kept her next comment to herself.

Elliot appeared then with a big sandwich.

Fiona looked at it and laughed. "If you can eat all that, you're doing pretty well."

Finn looked at the sandwich in shock. "Good Lord," but Elliot sat down beside him with one of equal size.

"I cut it in half in case you can't eat it all," Elliot said. He picked up his first half and chomped his way through it.

Finn looked at the food, looked at the ladies and said, "I'm not used to eating this much."

"Your body needs the nutrients," Fiona said. "Go ahead and eat. I'll talk to you later." And she turned and walked away.

As she did, she glanced back, caught Dani's eyes and smiled.

Dani always worried about everybody in the place, but those she knew personally before coming here she worried about even more.

Fiona didn't know why she was worried about Finn. What was going on with Finn that she either didn't like or didn't think Finn would like?

Chapter 2

F IONA APPEARED SHORTLY thereafter for her shift,
bright and cheerful as always. She'd enjoyed her week
off, but something about getting back home again felt so
right. She really loved working here, loved the people, both
staff and patients. It was always upsetting to come back and
find that somebody had left, and that was the case this time.
She studied the charts, looked over at Mina and asked,
"What happened to Fred's chart?"

Mina smiled and said, "He took an early discharge.
Transferred to his hometown. He and his girlfriend are now
engaged, and he wanted to be closer." Her tone was so
delighted that Fiona realized it was good news all around.

"I'm sorry I didn't get a chance to say goodbye," she exclaimed. "I really liked him."

"And he really liked you too," Mina said, sorting
through paperwork. "I think he left you a note. Aha." She
pulled out an envelope with Fiona's name on the front. "He
did."

Fiona smiled and reached for it, pulled out the folded
piece of paper and read out loud the few lines. "*Dear Fiona, I
wouldn't have come as far without your help or your care.
Thanks so much for holding my hand on the days when I
couldn't hold my own. Much love and progress in your bright
future.*" Fiona showed it to Mina. "Isn't it nice when we have

success stories?" she said.

Mina nodded and tapped the note. "You should frame that," she said in all seriousness. "That's a lovely goodbye."

"I know," Fiona said as she folded it and tucked it away in her pocket. "I'll figure out what to do with it later. But I'm back to work and reporting as scheduled," she said with a chuckle. She waved goodbye and headed into the nurses' station. She was still a couple minutes early, and that was good because she could catch up with her new patients and see about the progress on the ones she had left behind. A week here when she was on duty often seemed to take forever from Monday to Friday, but, when she was gone, it seemed like so much happened that it always shocked her. She walked in and smiled at Anna. "Hey there," she said. "How are you doing?"

"I'm doing just fine," Anna said, smiling. "And don't you look all bright and cheerful."

"Hey, a week off, you know what that's like."

"Not enough," Anna said, laughing. "But I leave on Monday."

"Right, I forgot about that," Fiona said. "In that case, you better catch me up before you leave because, after it starts to get busy here, I may not see you again today."

With that, they sat down with the stack of files and went through the progress on the patients. They split up the center by hallways and tried to keep a fairly even workload per nurse, but everybody always had one patient who caused trouble. It wasn't the same trouble that they would often have in a normal hospital because everybody was here by choice, but there were still problematic people. It didn't matter where you went or what setting you were in, there would almost always be at least *one*.

Anna tapped the top file and said, "So, this is Jerry. He was admitted last Monday, the first day you left. He's progressing and adapting slowly. As you can see, he's got extensive physical issues, and we haven't started his physiotherapy yet because, as soon as he arrived, he had a medical setback. He has pulled through at the moment, so, outside of keeping a tight watch and making sure the medications are working, the doctors are on it. By Monday we can start him on physiotherapy."

Fiona nodded thoughtfully. "It's funny how that happens, isn't it? They get here all excited, and then it seems, in some cases, they have a complete relapse, and it's back to the beginning again."

"I wonder how much of it is all the shock and excitement of getting here or how much effort it took and if it was too much for the body," Anna said. "The thing is, he's doing fine now."

"And I see we have another new patient today," Fiona said.

Anna smiled. "Yes. Finn, he's a friend of Dani's. He's also a friend of Elliot's."

"I just had coffee with them. Or, I should say, I just met them while they were all having coffee," she said. "So, Elliot, I presume, gave us a good reference to bring Finn in, and Dani, being the friend that she is, found him a spot."

"Dani always tries to get everybody in who asks," Anna said. "You know that."

"She does, indeed. And it seems like she and Aaron are making a go of it, so I'm really happy for her. But, of course, her heart is so big, all she wants to do is help heal the world."

"We need more people like her," Anna said. "Just think how much nicer the world would be to live in if we had people like her running the country."

Fiona chuckled. "Can you imagine?" she said. "Then again, we would all be healthy. We'd all be educated. We'd be treating each other nicely. And the world is so not like that."

Anna looked at her watch and said, "I'll introduce you to Jerry, and then we'll see how Finn has settled in."

"Sounds good," Fiona said as she picked up her stack of files, put them on the table and then took her tablet. "I'm sure glad we're digital here. I hear from friends in other places where they're really behind and nobody wants to spend the budget money and pieces of paper are all over the place."

"Well, we do both, don't we?" Anna said, "We have paper and digital, but I think digital is the way of the future. It also helps keep track of what the doctors are up to."

"True enough," Fiona said. "Sometimes I wish I'd become a doctor."

"Not me," Anna said. "This is the level I'm happiest at. I'm great as a supporting staff, but I wouldn't want to be the one making the frontline decisions."

Fiona chuckled. "I hear you there," she said. "So maybe I'm happy as a nurse and not a doctor after all."

They walked into Jerry's room to find him dressed and lying on top of his covers.

Fiona smiled and said, "That's always a good sign."

Anna walked up and greeted him gently. "I see you had a bit of a rough weekend," she said.

He glanced up at her smile and said, "It's nothing compared to when I first arrived. I was just trying to not do too much again."

Fiona stepped up, gave him a finger shake and said,

"You should know better by now," she said.

He grinned at her and said, "You're new."

She nodded. "I'm Fiona. I was gone for a week's holiday, but I'm back now, and I'll be taking over for Anna."

Immediately his smile fell away, and he glanced at Anna. "Where are you going?"

"I'm on holiday starting Monday," she said cheerfully. "Don't worry though. I'll be back the following Monday."

"Well, I can tell you right now," he said, "I'll still be here." And then he laughed and laughed.

Fiona grinned. "Glad to see you have such a great sense of humor," she said. She quickly took his vitals, and, when she checked his blood pressure, she frowned.

He shook his head at her. "Don't tell the doc," he said, "but I had some potato chips yesterday, and that salt always sends my blood pressure way up."

"Then you know not to eat them, don't you?" she said, putting the note down on her file.

He watched her and frowned. "Are you tattling on me?"

"If you ate so many that your blood pressure's affected, yes," she said with a serene smile. "Next time, show some restraint and have half the amount."

With Jerry still protesting, they walked out of the room to his laughter. In the hallway, Fiona said, "Where's he getting that stash of potato chips from?"

"We'll have to talk to the kitchen," Anna said. "He's definitely got a weight issue that we need to work on too."

"Yeah, that's slowing his progress. Physiotherapy will have a heyday with him."

"Let's hope he has some fun and us too," Anna said, and that set the tone for the rest of the morning as they went through everybody in their quarter. By the time they made it back to the nurses' station, Fiona felt like she'd never left.

"Why don't you get your lunch first?" Anna asked. "I'll go afterward."

"Sounds good," Fiona said. Then she stopped and said, "We didn't go to Finn's room."

"No, he's being assessed by the doctors all morning," Anna said. "We'll have to tackle him after lunch."

"Right," she said. She headed to the kitchen, but so many people were there that she thought maybe, just maybe, she would push that back a little bit and grab something to eat at her desk when Anna was gone.

With that thought in mind, she escaped the crowd and headed downstairs into the veterinarian clinic. She walked into the main reception area to see Mavis sitting there.

Mavis took one look, stood and opened her arms. Fiona chuckled and gave the woman a big hug. "It seems like you've been gone forever," Mavis said.

"Oh, no," Fiona said. "Just a week. And right now, it feels like I never even got that."

"There's nothing like leaving, but, when you come back, there's nothing like being home again," Mavis said comfortably. "Stan is just about to take a break if you want to have a coffee with him."

"If he's around," she said, "I'd love to see him."

At that, Stan stepped out, saying goodbye to another patient. Fiona chuckled as a Chihuahua walked forward stiffly, eager to get away from the vet. She looked at him, and Stan grinned at her. "Welcome back."

"What happened to the little guy?" she asked, motioning at the woman leading the Chihuahua out to the parking lot.

"Greenstick fracture on the back leg," he explained. "He'll be fine."

"I haven't seen Chickie since I came back," she said. "Granted, I've only been on my corner all morning, but I miss the little guy."

"Chickie and Helga are doing fine," Stan said. "Plus, we have a couple new recruits here too."

"Ones staying or ones you're fostering?" she asked curiously.

He walked her down the hallway toward the barn. Stan stopped at one of the horse stalls, and there in front of her was a small llama. She stared at it and cried out, "Oh my."

"She was surrendered to one of the animal centers," he said, "and they were trying to find somebody to keep her when one of Dani's friends called here." He gave her a lopsided grin. "For some reason, Dani seems to think this little girl belongs here."

"How old is she?"

"That's the problem," he said. "She's only six months old, and she's fairly attached to this guy." He pointed deeper into the stall at an Appaloosa horse. Fiona looked at him, and he said, "Yes, they were raised together. This one is two years old, but, ever since the llama came to visit, the two have been inseparable."

"And anybody with a horse that needs a home, of course, Dani's all over it," she said, laughing.

"When it came with a sidekick like this one, absolutely."

"And what are their names?"

Stan laughed and laughed. "Well, the Appaloosa is, of course, named Appie," he said, "because people are so original. And the llama? ... Can you guess?"

She looked at him, stared and said, "Oh, please no. Not Lammie?"

He shook his head and laughed. "It's almost as bad. Her

name is Lovely."

"Oh, that's lovely," she said.

The llama's ears twitched. She looked right at Fiona and took several hesitant steps toward Stan, who opened the stall door and motioned for Fiona to come inside. "She's very friendly."

"What about Appie?" she asked, eyeing the big gelding a little more warily. "He might be young, but he's big."

"Yes, something else is in his heritage," he said. "Appaloosa, of course, refers to the coloring and the breed but generally not of this size. And he's young, so he's potentially still not done growing." He crouched in front of Lovely and gently stroked her long neck and scratched around her ears.

"So how long do they have to stay in the stall?" she asked. "It's a beautiful sunny day. I imagine they want out."

He laughed. "That's what I was just about to do on my lunch hour. We'll put them in a pen by themselves and see how they adjust first before we mix them in with the other horses." He held up a halter, which he quickly slipped over Lovely's nose and face. "Do you want to take Lovely out?" He walked over to Appie, hooked a lead to his halter and walked out into the front pasture. Appie wasn't too sure about going until he saw Lovely following him.

Fiona marveled at the bond between the two, yet it was just like humans. Everything was easier if you weren't alone. Out into the sunshine they stepped, and she followed Stan as he led Appie to one of the pastures close by. Just as she was about to join him, she heard sounds of a wheelchair.

She turned to look, and there was Dani with Finn. Fiona stopped and smiled. "Finn, you want to meet this guy?"

Finn said, "Sure."

Dani called out, "I do. Stan, are they ready to go out to

the pasture?"

He nodded and brought Appie over to be introduced as well. Appie behaved himself beautifully, bending down to let Finn gently rub his nose.

"He's beautiful," Finn said sincerely. And then he looked at the llama and smiled. "But there is beautiful, and then there's absolutely adorable."

Stan quickly explained their ages and the medical problems each had. But Finn was head-over-heels in love, cuddling little Lovely. "Hard to believe she'll grow to be the same size as Appie here."

Stan said, "Not quite the same, but close."

Finn looked at the little one, then up at the big horse and shook his head. "It's almost a shame. She's so adorable right now."

They walked them to the pasture, with Finn and Dani watching, and then took off the leads, leaving the halters on.

"Shouldn't we take it off the little one?" Fiona worried about the material chafing the baby's skin.

"Yes, you can take it off Lovely," he said. "They're quite easy to catch, apparently."

Dani walked in, leaving Finn sitting in the wheelchair just off to the side. She walked up, unclipped the halter from Appie. "It's best for him to get used to being free and to trust us in that way too," she said, handing the halter to Stan. She reached up scratched Appie along the face where the halter had rested.

Appie nuzzled her gently and then took a few steps away. Realizing he had his freedom, he danced off to the side, then picked up steam and ran. Lovely immediately followed. They raced around the pasture several times before slowly coming to a walk and strolling toward the group of people again.

Stan stood beside Dani and said, "Let's hope they were right about being easy to catch."

"If not, we'll bring in a wrangler." Dani laughed, stretching out an arm to encompass the nearby pastures where her other horses—Midnight, Molly and Maggie—grazed contentedly. "But we know that trust is everything. Especially here."

FINN LISTENED TO her words and realized that Dani really was living what she believed. He wanted to believe it would have the same effect on him that it had on Elliot, and Finn could already see that Appie was amazed at his newfound freedom. Lovely was just beyond adorable though. He watched and smiled at the llama's antics as it dashed under Appie's belly and came up on the other side. The two of them played, danced around and nuzzled, and, when Dani whistled, Appie came immediately.

She scratched him on the face and said, "Good boy." She gave him a treat that she must have had in her pocket and then watched as Stan fed him a few more. They then gave Lovely a couple treats more suited to llamas.

Dani stepped out of the pasture, turned and said, "Go and enjoy, guys."

Appie, realizing he was once again free, took off with Lovely at his side. Finn stared at the two animals, realizing just how much mobility played into everybody's life. He stared at his missing leg and thought about all the things that he had bitched about and how absolutely meaningless they were at this point in time. He knew he could get a prosthetic that would fit, particularly after the surgery he just had. It would take a bit, and he'd have to start with some pretty rough stuff, but he knew he'd get there. And, just like Appie and Lovely ahead of him, he was pretty darn sure he could enjoy the same freedom with the same exuberance that they had just shown.

Dani walked over and smiled at Finn. "Aren't they beautiful?" she exclaimed, her face bright and so happy.

He nodded and smiled back. "They are, indeed."

Just then his gaze caught on Fiona's face as she stared at the animals racing across the green hills. There was such a serenity and a deep sense of contentment on her face. Whereas Dani's expression was full of joy, Fiona's was different, a quieter happiness. He smiled up at her. "You two are both so lovely," he said. "Don't think I've seen any women more beautiful."

Fiona laughed. "That's the Blarney Stone you've been kissing."

He grinned at her. "I thought you would be my nurse," he said, "but I've yet to see you."

"We were at your room this morning," she said, "or at least you were on my roster, but I understood you were still consulting with the doctors. But, if you're done, we can always start after lunch."

"Lunch," he said in mock horror. "Have I missed it?"

"No," she said, "I haven't had mine either."

Dani motioned at Finn and asked, "Fiona, would you mind taking him through the cafeteria then? I've got to get to my office for a meeting at one." She waved goodbye and quickly dashed off.

"She's special, isn't she?" Fiona asked, watching Dani run off.

He beamed up at her. "She always has been," he said.

"And a very good friend. I'm blessed."

"We all are," she said, motioning to Stan, who was still standing and staring at the horses. "Whether four-legged animals or two-legged humans," she said, "we've all been blessed by Dani's vision."

"Do you know the major?" he asked. "I knew him when I was friends with Dani a long time ago, but he was a pretty difficult person back then."

"Well, that's changed too," Fiona said, stepping behind Finn and pushing the wheelchair. "Now let's get some lunch. Then we can start with you afterward."

"Oh, is it back to business already?" he asked with a mock grin.

"Everything here is blended," she said, "some business and some pleasure."

"Right. Well, I am hungry," he admitted. "The thing is, I hate eating."

"Yeah, because of the colostomy?"

He sank inward slightly and then realized that, as his nurse, of course, she'd seen his file. He nodded slowly. "It's very unsexy," he announced.

At that, she laughed and laughed.

And yet, he didn't feel like she was laughing at him. He twisted to look up at her. "It's not *that* funny," he said crossly.

"Nope," she said, "it's not that funny. It's the way you said it, as if that was the epitome of your world's woes right now," she said. "I can think of a lot of things that could be so much worse."

"I know, and, in a place like this, I feel bad for bitching," he said. "I'm sure other guys with colostomies are here too." He looked at her hopefully.

She smiled but didn't say anything.

He sighed. "It's pretty bad to realize now how much that's bothered me. But I don't know why."

"It's a fact of life," she said calmly. "You took major damage to your intestines and your colon, so that's part of it. The fact that we have medical surgeries that can fix it so you can still function as a normal, healthy human being and still eat normally," she said, "that's another miracle."

"And the leg?"

She just waved her hand.

He realized that, for her, it was just that simple.

"You'll fix that in no time," she said. "I understand you recently had surgery, and the stump is pretty raw because they had to go in and make a few changes to the blood vessels and the tendons. It will make life so much easier when you get a proper prosthetic. Once you're standing on your own two feet," she said, "the change, mentally and emotionally, is amazing."

He nodded slowly. "I felt that the one or two times when I was being fitted. To be able to walk ... Humans weren't meant to always be sitting," he admitted. "And just something about taking back control ..."

"Exactly," she said. "However, in your case, I would think your back is the bigger issue."

At that, he fell silent. "I try to ignore it," he said. "I haven't started PT yet, so ..."

"And you'll hate your therapists at the beginning," she said, her voice calm but cheerful. "But they'll make for an incredible difference at the end of it all."

"We can't strengthen what is gone, though," he said. "So there are no miracles in my world."

"You'd be surprised how the body can compensate," Fiona said. "So come on. Let's see if we can fill that colostomy bag."

Chapter 3

FIONA GRINNED AT Finn's response, but she was serious; there were things in life to be worried about, and there were others that just weren't worth all that energy. He had a lot to learn here, but, at the end of the day, his priorities would be realigned, and he'd be happy. Getting him there, well, maybe not so much.

She understood another aspect. Everybody assumed that because they were in a rehab center like this that only the residents had health issues, and that wasn't the case. Several of the staff had health challenges of their own. But it wasn't the time or the place for that discussion. Finn wasn't ready to hear about anybody else because he was still stuck on *poor me.*

Just wanting to know that he wasn't alone with a colostomy bag was one of those signs. He needed to know that he wasn't the only one who's had such a hard time. She thought a colostomy bag was a huge invention and a medical step forward, and it was so much easier to deal with than he likely realized. But he would over time. This was still new to him.

Back upstairs at the cafeteria she pushed him into the line and said, "Do you want to try this yourself, or do you want help?"

He looked at her and said, "Well, I can't reach the tray, so maybe you could help me with that."

"Gotcha." She put the tray down for him and then walked with him.

As they walked along, he said, "Is there a menu?"

She pointed up to the back wall. He stared up at it and said, "Wow, okay, I want pierogis and cabbage rolls."

On the back side of the counter, Dennis, according to the name tag on his T-shirt, smiled at Finn and said, "Hey, you're new."

Finn grinned. "Are you here so much that you recognize everybody?"

"Been here since Hathaway House opened," he said with a big smirk. "I know every one of you guys. And I'll get your favorites down pretty darn fast."

"Well, that would not be hard," he said. "My favorites are cinnamon buns and a good steak."

Dennis chuckled. "That just makes you male," he said. "Now, what can I get you for lunch?"

Finn quickly gave his order and watched as a huge amount of food was put on his plate. Finn tried to stop Dennis. "Whoa, that's way too much for me."

Dennis looked down and raised an eyebrow but handed over the plate as he said, "Now there's more food, lots of coffee, lots of desserts. Keep moving down the line and grab what you want." He flashed a big grin at Fiona and served her about half the portion he'd given Finn.

Fiona moved Finn along the line to the tea and coffee and asked, "Do you want something to drink now, or do you want it later?"

"I'd love some water," he said, studying the large cooler's selection of cold drinks in front of him.

She pointed ahead and said, "Go grab one."

Dennis came around from the back and said, "Let me

grab the tray for you."

They waited while Finn awkwardly wheeled up to the cooler and tried to open the door. It took several attempts to open it without the wheelchair being in the way, and, at the time, he appeared frustrated and flustered, as if wondering why no one was helping him.

As Fiona and Dennis watched, she smiled and whispered, "Gotta love it when they start."

"It's always tough, isn't it?

They watched as Finn finally pulled back enough to figure out how to open up the door and then wheeled around and grabbed the water, and, just because he was in there, he grabbed three.

Dennis chuckled. "I can see this guy'll make sure he gets what he wants when he wants it."

She smiled, walked past Finn and said, "Come on. Let's go this way. We'll sit outside."

She didn't give him a chance to argue and headed for a table that was half in the sun and half out. She put her tray down, waited for him to roll up beside her, and she asked, "Which side do you want? Sun or without?"

"No sun," he said briskly.

She nodded and removed the chair so he could sit easier. Dennis placed the other tray down, and she sat across from Finn. She grabbed one of the bottles of water and asked, "May I?"

He stared at her resentfully.

She grinned and said, "Around here, the more you can do yourself, the better off you are. Yes, it took you several times to make it, but that's not the issue. Celebrate the wins. You accomplished your task, and you did it very quickly. I was impressed."

He looked at her in surprise, and then, as if realizing she was serious, he smiled, grabbed a bottle of water for himself and said, "I did, didn't I?" He grinned and held up his bottle, and they tapped them together, saying, "Cheers."

FINN HAD TO smile. He hadn't realized just how affected he was by being watched—or, in this case, by appearing stupid, awkward and like he couldn't do anything. It was a completely different thing being in a rehab center like this where everybody appeared to be in similar circumstances. When he was in the hospital, everybody jumped to help. And maybe that hadn't been the best thing for him, but it had been easy and stress-free. The last thing he needed was extra stress.

But somehow he didn't think that same let-me-help-you philosophy would work here. It seemed to him that Fiona watching him and waiting for him to deal with it in that calm, unfazed manner of hers showed a lot about who she was. He wasn't sure that he liked it, but he admired it. He also admired that she didn't seem to care whether he approved or not.

She smiled at him. "Not quite what you were expecting, was it?"

He shook his head quietly. "No. I'm used to people jumping up and helping."

"I get that," she said cheerfully. "But think about the advantages of us not doing that."

He frowned at her, but her grin widened. His shoulders sagged as he agreed. "I still don't like feeling like a fool."

She stared at him, her gaze gentle. "The only fool is a fool who doesn't try," she said.

His brows came together as he thought about that. "I'm sure there's something very philosophical about that," he muttered. "But I'm not really seeing it."

She smiled. "Appearances matter to you, don't they? You have this view of who you are and what you should be, and, anything different than that, you're not willing to accept."

"Is anybody?" he asked, wanting to challenge her on that. He shifted uncomfortably. "Besides, you're my nurse, not my shrink."

She settled back and looked around.

He wondered if he'd hurt her and immediately felt bad. "I'm sorry," he muttered.

"No need to be."

"Yes, there is," he said. "I didn't mean to come across as an arrogant asshole. Apparently, I've been doing a little bit too much of that lately."

"Or, you are somebody desperate for the same chance that you see everybody else getting," she murmured. "The thing is, when you're desperate, it doesn't happen."

Her words were like a sock to his gut because so much truth was behind them, but how did she know? He stared down at his water bottle, wondering.

"Everybody comes here with that same look," she explained, her voice once again cool but warm. "And you have every right to it. This is your life. This is your physical body. This is your future. You have to want this change, to be the best you can be. You have to be hungry for it," she said. "But you have to be willing to do the work to get there. And the work is not always the work that you think it'll be."

He stared back at her. He didn't even necessarily want to go down that train of thought. But what she was offering him was tantalizing. "Is that part of your shrink duties?" he asked, but he tried to keep the sarcasm out of it.

"We're all shrinks here," she said, "because we're all people who walk this world called life. None of us are any better than you. None of us are any worse. We're all here on this journey. We're all at different stages. Just because I'm healthy and seemingly whole and have a job where I get to help people become healthy and whole doesn't mean I'm ahead of you. On the contrary," she said, "I've learned so much on a day-to-day basis from each and every one of you that I know that I'm further behind."

She almost took his breath away. He took a sip, trying to gather his thoughts as he considered her words. "I guess you've seen it all, haven't you?"

"I keep thinking I have, and then I get a new patient with a new set of problems and a new set of beliefs and a new set of handicaps, and I realize that, yet again, somebody new with something different has presented which I haven't seen before, and it's another opportunity to learn."

Her words were hard-hitting, and yet, so damn meaningful that it made him feel small. "It seems like, every time you open your mouth right now, you come out with something incredibly prophetic, and it makes me feel even smaller," he admitted. "I had no idea my insecurity was such an issue."

"What I've found," she said in a conversational tone, leaning forward and linking her fingers loosely in front of her, "is that whenever we're up against a new challenge—in your case, your physical disabilities—it makes us all feel very insecure because it's different. We don't experience a stable footing to stand on. We don't know what we're up against, so we don't have the confidence to know if we can handle it. It's as if the mountain seems to be so big that you just don't have the coping skills, so everything falls apart. And the first thing to go is your sense of confidence, your sense of security, your ability *to do* versus *maybe I can do*." She cut her roll in half and offered him half.

He stared at it and then nodded. He leaned forward, wincing only a little at his back as it twinged with the movement.

"Did you lose that kidney too?" she asked, her tone so normal and commonplace.

He laughed and said, "I did. That and a bunch of other stuff." He picked up the half of her roll, took a bite and slowly savored it.

She nodded and said, "You haven't allowed yourself much in the way of food, have you?"

Instinctively he gazed at his waist.

She nodded, "Because whatever goes in has to come out, and you've been avoiding what comes out."

He flushed, looking around, wishing she kept her voice low.

"If I were to stand on this tabletop and yell out to everybody that you have a colostomy bag," she said comfortably, "not one person here would give a shit or be fazed by it."

"How do you know?" he asked in horrified fascination. "Do you do that to all the newbies who come here?"

She stared at him in surprise for a moment and then went off in a peal of laughter. When she finally calmed down, she wiped the tears from her eyes, still chuckling, and said, "Oh, that was great," she said. "No, I don't. I should though, shouldn't I?" Still chuckling, she checked her watch and said, "Not sure what time your next appointment is, but I have to get going."

"What time is it?" he asked.

"One."

He nodded. "I should go too. I'm not exactly sure how anything works here, but it seems like it's not really been set up yet."

"That's normal until everybody on the team gets up to speed," she said, standing. "Do you want a hand back?"

"I think the answer that I'm supposed to give you," he said, "is, *No, I'll do it myself.* But the honest truth is, I would. I'm quite tired." He lifted a hand to see it trembling.

She gave a decisive nod. "I'm taking my lunch back to my desk. Let's get your drink and your lunch and bring it back with you." She quickly packed up a tray, put it on his lap, walked behind him, pushing him toward his room.

"Are you supposed to see me this afternoon?"

"Yes, I am," she said. "Will you be there, or will you run away?"

"I was thinking that I really wanted to see you," he said. "You have a take on life that's refreshing."

"It's because I like to take life by the hand and give it a good shake and see what falls out," she said, still laughing.

"Like I said, refreshing."

Chapter 4

A S SOON AS Fiona got Finn back to his room, with assurances that he was fully capable of getting onto his bed and that he should lay here and close his eyes for a bit, she placed his tray of food on the night table and headed back to the nurses' station with her lunch. She was still chuckling about his comment, asking if that's how she introduced all newbies to the center, because it wasn't a bad idea.

From the very start, get over the embarrassment, get over that humiliation, get over the unseen worry that people were whispering behind their backs, so that everybody knew upfront exactly what the problem was, and then they could get on with it. They could move past all the initial hurdles with a modicum of effort.

She was all about being transparent, about being out-spoken, but she'd learned that one had to tread carefully because most men's egos were fragile. She'd also found that men made the worst patients if they still expected to be a big, strong, hunky he-man type.

In this place, sometimes they needed to cry like a baby. Sometimes the fear, the worries, the pain were just too much for the he-man image. They broke down, and they always felt embarrassed afterward. They always felt like they had somehow broken some male pledge to be strong forever. It took time for them to adjust to the fact that this was normal behavior and that not everybody could be strong all the time. Not only that but it sometimes took the strongest of men to let out that pain, let out that grief, so they could wake up the next day and start all over again.

She'd seen some of the PT sessions that were absolutely, unbearably painful. And it was her job to help ease that pain in whatever way she could so that the patient could get up the next day and do it all over again. Eventually, over time, it got easier. Eventually, over time, the pain diminished; and eventually, over time, they didn't need her. That was both a sad and a great moment. Because they could sleep on their own then. Having seen the progress, having seen that momentous change was the tipping point in their recovery.

Everybody went through a process, but everybody's process was different. It's not enough to think that everybody processed things differently, because, of course, they did, but everybody experienced things differently too. That meant everybody's tipping point was different.

Wouldn't it be nice if she could say, "Five days of doing this and you'll hit that tipping point. When you wake up on day six, it'll be as if you scaled that mountain. You'll feel like you are David who killed Goliath." But it wasn't like that. Sometimes the tipping point came at six months; sometimes it came at three months, and sometimes, for some people, it took years.

She'd had one patient who was here for six months. He went home not quite as healed as much as they all expected for him, and, when he came back almost a year and a half later, he'd walked into the center as a visitor, visibly healed in body and mind. Not in a wheelchair but standing straight and tall, wearing casual jeans and a T-shirt, and she'd been shocked and delighted to see him. She'd walked forward, held out her hand, shook his and said, "Wow."

He grinned and said, "And that's why I came back. When I left, I was a mess, and I wasn't ready to listen to anything you had to say. I wasn't ready to hear anything you wanted me to hear. I was a slow learner. But I did get the message—finally. I'm here in town, and I deliberately made this trip just so I could see you and could let you know that I finally found that tipping point. For *me*."

Tears had come to her eyes, and she'd flung herself into his arms and hugged him hard. It had been mutual, and, when he'd left, there had been more tears in his eyes too, but he'd become a whole man, a healthy man, and she'd never ever seen anything better.

Even now she could feel the tears in her eyes, that sense of joy, that beautiful sense of accomplishment of knowing that that broken man had reached that point in time. They still corresponded. He was back out West again. She knew that she wasn't important in his life now, but she'd been important then, and she'd been important up to the point that he had needed her to be. And, once he didn't need her anymore, he'd moved on, and that was the way it should be.

Was it her fault that she gave a little bit of her heart to each and every one of her patients? Maybe that's why she had no relationship now—because she'd given away so many pieces of her heart to these men who had shown her just what a real man was.

She didn't want the jocks. She didn't want the slick businessmen, and she certainly didn't want the successful millionaires because money didn't matter. She saw money here every damn day. Money made no difference because money didn't give you the spirit to get up in the morning.

Money didn't give you the courage to crawl out of bed to face PT when you knew it would hurt and it would send you crawling back in tears, wishing you could die so you didn't have to face another day. Money didn't do a damn bit of good when you had to crawl inside yourself to find out who you really were, because, at the end of the day, we were all poor unless we had built up our own riches, and we had that bank account of self-reliance to draw on in times of need.

Like the real men she'd seen here had done.

That was the kind of man she wanted.

TWO DAYS LATER Finn slowly worked himself out of bed and did several loosening-up exercises, as he'd been instructed. When he was done, he pulled out his tablet to check what was on his list today. As he sorted it out in his head, he dropped into his wheelchair, headed to the bathroom, quickly went through his morning ritual. By the time he made his way back to the bed, he could already feel a sense of exhaustion. He was never big on routine. It was necessary for many parts of life, but he'd always found it was a difficult thing for him to get into in his personal life.

But he didn't have much choice here. He literally tapped items off his list as he went through everything, and the list was extensive, as if they knew that he might skip one of every two items on his list. He also knew that tablet sent the same tally in real-time so that everybody else on his team could see what he'd done—or tried or skipped—at any time.

Sure, he could lie and tap and say he'd done all these things, but that wasn't who he was. And just staring at the list was both empowering and terrifying.

He slowly dressed, wondering when he could get fitted for another prosthetic. That would make a huge difference to his mental state. He stared at the wheelchair and wondered if he was ready to go with crutches. He'd done a lot of work on crutches before, but his back ...

He grabbed the crutches and walked to the doorway, awkwardly opening it, and stepped out. He took several deep breaths as he looked around and realized that the cafeteria hadn't looked quite so far away when he was in his wheelchair, but, now that he was on crutches, it looked miles away. It shouldn't matter. He'd been there and back many times. It was amazing how being on crutches made the world look different. Still, he figured he could go for breakfast, maybe not make a fool of himself, then could come back and switch into the wheelchair for his first PT session.

He wasn't looking forward to it, and he was waffling as to whether he should even eat beforehand. The last thing he wanted was the embarrassment of having this colostomy bag filling while he was in a PT session, and yet, he knew it probably wouldn't be the first time for his therapist. It would just be Finn's first time. Muttering, "There will be a lot of first times coming up," he slowly worked his way to the cafeteria, happy to feel his body getting into the swing of things a little easier than he thought. But he also knew how damn easy it was to overdo things.

At the cafeteria, he'd managed to get a tray off the stack and onto the runner, and, as he hobbled along, he saw Dennis at the end. He beamed when he saw the crutches. "Moving up in the world, are you?"

Finn grinned back at the wonderfully even-tempered man and said, "Maybe, but I could fall flat on my face trying to get to a table with a full tray."

"I've got your back there, not a problem. What can I get you for breakfast?"

Finn settled on a nice omelet stuffed with veggies, a big glass of juice and a little bit of fruit. As he got his tray to the coffee station, he studied the tray and wondered how he would ever make that trip to the table. He'd seen others do it easily enough, but he figured he'd dump everything on the floor.

While he was still frowning, Dennis came, snatched the tray from in front of him and said, "Lead on."

Laughing, he hobbled his way forward so he was out on the deck again. Dennis placed the tray on the table in front of him and said, "Enjoy."

He disappeared without giving Finn a chance to even say thank-you, but he called it out anyway. Just because Dennis couldn't hear it didn't mean Finn didn't need to thank him for the help. He laughed because he figured that was also something that Fiona would agree with. That thought uppermost, he tucked into his breakfast and settled back with his coffee. He was thinking a refill would be really nice, but it was too damn far away. He watched as some other guy walked with a tray, while on two crutches and talking to his buddy. Amazingly the man made it to his table, sat down and never spilled a drop. Finn shook his head in amazement.

"You'll be doing that in no time," a familiar voice said.

He looked up to see Fiona walking toward him, two cups of coffee in her hand.

He grinned and asked, "Is one of those for me?"

"It so is," she said with a grin. She motioned to the man he'd watched. "Don't worry. You'll be doing that soon too. It just takes time and practice."

"I can't imagine," he said. "Dennis helped me this morning."

"Dennis will help you anytime you need it," she said. "He's a very giving person."

"He is, at that," Finn said. "I was figuring out whether I should eat before therapy or not."

"It's your first session?"

"Well, we've done the testing," he said with a half nod. "Today is the start of the exercises."

"Well, they won't go too crazy on you then," she said. "I'll stop by afterward at the end of my shift to see how you're holding up."

"So you can cheer me on or hold my hand in commiseration?"

"To see if you need pain meds," she corrected with a half laugh.

He winced at that. "It'll be bad, won't it?"

"Maybe not," she said. "But, if you didn't need help, you wouldn't be here."

"It's my back," he admitted.

"It won't be just your back then," she said. "Once a muscle is damaged, other muscles are called into play. In this case, you've got a lot of back injuries that pretty well affect your entire body."

"Right," he nodded. "And what do I do if I have an accident?" he asked bluntly. There was silence for a moment. He glanced up to see her studying him and again found that warm glow. He flushed. "Yes, I'm worried about humiliating myself," he muttered. "Yes, I'm worried about acting like a fool. And, yes, I'm afraid of making a mess and having to get help," he said. "Is that so wrong?"

"Not only is it *not* wrong," she said, "I'm really happy you managed to voice that."

He could feel the heat getting stronger on his cheeks. He shrugged uncomfortably.

She chuckled. "And, like so many men, you don't like to talk about such things."

"No," he said, "I prefer to avoid those conversations than to talk about them."

"So you can either tell your therapist that you have a colostomy bag, so that you're both not surprised, or you can expect that they will have done their job and will have read your chart," she said firmly, "and will be expecting that bag to be there and will also be working on the muscles that are required to keep the bag functioning properly."

"I don't know how much is required," he muttered. "I'm just worrying."

"About leakage?" she asked.

He hated to even discuss it, but he nodded quietly.

"And again, doing the exercises, you could find that is a problem."

"Which is exactly why I brought it up," he said. "You know, if it was a guy I was talking to now, it wouldn't be quite so bad."

At that, she laughed. "We have lots of male therapists," she said, "but I don't think you'll be that lucky."

Finn groaned and asked, "Why?"

"Because you have one of our new therapists. She's tiny. She's bouncy. She's bubbly, and she's got a mean streak in her."

He stared at Fiona in shock. "So that really won't help my cause, will it?"

"Part of being here is to get adjusted and to be happy and to understand where you are physically," she said. "You cannot hide from this forever."

"I don't want to hide from it," he said. "I want to hide *it* from everyone else."

She nodded. "Heard and understood. But don't expect miracles."

And then, realizing the time, he struggled to his feet, grabbed his crutches and said, "Wish me luck."

"You won't need it," she said in a gentle tone of voice. "Remember. It's a bodily function, and it's also one of the greatest gifts you got. That surgery saved your life. Learn to work with it, not against it." And, on that note, she sat back and sipped her coffee.

Chapter 5

F IONA STOPPED BY late in the afternoon to find Finn in his room, sitting on his bed, despondent, covered in sweat and looking like hell. She rapped on the open door and stepped inside.

He looked up at her, flashed her a half smile and said, "If you want conversation, I don't have it in me." He shifted on the bed and collapsed flat, his head on his pillow. "I'm done," he whispered. "Just bury me now."

She chuckled out loud. "If I had a dollar for every time I heard a patient say something similar ..."

He lifted a hand and waved it at her. "I know. You'd be a millionaire by now, right?"

"Absolutely," she whispered. "So, do you need pain meds."

"Well, I don't know," he said. "It's more muscle cramps than pain."

"Where?" she asked, stepping to his side.

He shifted, rolled over until he was sideways and said, "My back."

She could actually see the knots cramping. He groaned as one spiked and bunched up under her fingers. She gently helped him so he lay on his stomach, then straightened out his frame so that she could get at the muscles and gently started massaging. Using pressure and tension, she pulled and stretched out the knots. When she was done, she asked, "Anything else?"

But there was no answer. She leaned over to see his breathing was strong and steady, his eyes closed. She smiled and stepped back. She'd check on him later and see if he needed anything. For the moment, what he really needed was rest and recuperation. He might also miss dinner, which may or may not be a good thing in this case. She headed to the cafeteria, grabbed herself a half sandwich and a salad and said to Dennis, "Finn crashed. He might be looking for food a bit later."

"Okay," he said. "It's always tough when they first get here, isn't it?"

"Sometimes I think it's tough right through to the day they leave," she admitted. She smiled, her gaze meeting Dennis's with the same understanding that he showed everybody else. He'd been here a long time, and so had she. Not quite as long but almost. Smiling, she took her dinner to a table and sat down.

Almost immediately Dani sat down beside her. She smiled at her friend.

"I hardly ever see you these days," Fiona said teasingly.

Dani just rolled her eyes. "We have so many people coming and going," she said. "It's getting crazy."

"Plus the addition in progress," Fiona reminded her friend.

"And the addition," Dani agreed. "How is Finn doing?" she asked bluntly.

Fiona smiled. "As far as I can tell, it's been a bit of a shock arriving here," she said carefully. "I just gave him a massage and helped him to crash. He had his first real PT this afternoon, and he's exhausted. I just warned Dennis that he might need food in a bit."

Dani's face immediately closed down, slightly pinched with worry. "He's been a good friend. I offered him a bed a while ago, but he wasn't ready."

"I'm not sure he's ready now either," she said bluntly, "but he's trying to get up to snuff fast."

"He's always been like that," Dani said. "Came from behind and took over very quickly. I know that he always had a bit of a self-confidence issue, so I think his injuries probably made it a lot worse."

"I think his colostomy bag is his biggest hang-up," Fiona said. "I've known several women with them, but I haven't really had personal experience with too many men."

"And yet, it's such a marvel of modern medicine," Dani said with a smile. "I guess it's that whole male-ego thing again, isn't it?"

"I would think so. But, as he becomes more comfortable dealing with the changes to his body, I think he'll become a little more comfortable around other people too."

"And, of course, being in a place like this, we're fairly blasé about it," Dani said. "But, for him, he's not quite to that level yet."

"No, but I think the faster he gets there, the better off he'll be," she said. "Bodily functions are bodily functions, and there isn't an easy way to deal with them when things mess up."

"Isn't that the truth," Dani said. "Maybe I'll check in on him after I eat and see how he's doing."

"And maybe take him back down to the animals, if you have a chance," Fiona said. "Or I should. Let's see how he is when he wakes up. I know he was pretty exhausted when I found him, not to mention had lots of muscle cramps."

"The animals are a huge help," Dani said with a tender smile as she looked across the deck. "Lovely is absolutely lovely," she emphasized.

"I think the animals would help Finn too. Animals are so very natural in their own skin," Fiona said. "It would make a massive difference if people could be the same."

"More than that," Dani said, "the more that he realizes we don't care about his supposed limitations and that we accept him for who he is, I think the better off he'll be all around."

"Only when he starts to accept it for himself," Fiona corrected. "Then he'll be perfect."

AS THE DAYS had gone by, Finn was wrapped up in this roller coaster of tears, burning depression, feelings of hopelessness. There were smaller triumphs too but also more defeats. Only his visits with Elliot kept Finn from sinking too deep. So far he'd kept the depth of his emotions from his friend, but it had been hard. Sometimes almost impossible.

When he woke up on his one-month anniversary, it almost blew him away with what he'd accomplished, but it highlighted just how much he still had yet to do. His team had spent the last few weeks doing one thing: strengthening a specific set of muscles in his back so that he could sit properly. He hadn't realized how much he was forcing the rest of his body to compensate for the weak muscles until they'd taken pictures and shown him how he slouched to the side while sitting.

He'd thought nothing of it, only that he was finding a comfortable spot. It was odd now, as if he were finding a place for all his organs so that they would rest naturally inside. He was missing a few parts, and others weren't quite the same anymore. It had never occurred to him how much overall adjustment was needed for that. But he'd managed for a half hour to sit straight, not even conscious of what he was doing, before he started to slump.

And then his therapist had come along and had given him a hard poke, reminding him that his posture was once again falling. He'd straightened but had hurt himself in the process. The only damn good thing about his time here were the massages.

That had to be the best benefit of being injured. He didn't know if other places did them, and he hadn't gotten anything like that at the hospital. But here, after a heavy workout, his therapist gave him a hard rubdown. Several times he'd had muscle cramps, and a couple times he'd fallen asleep on her.

He'd been embarrassed at the time, but she never said anything, making him realize she was used to that reaction. Same with Fiona. It almost made him sad. He wanted to be special, and yet, he didn't want to be special in a needy way. He didn't want to be special in an injured way. He wanted to be like a special man. And all that seemed so damn far away. He wasn't even sure it was something he could feel.

When Fiona came in that morning and took his blood pressure, she frowned at it and said, "Looks like you didn't wake up on the right side of the bed."

"Just woke up feeling a little bit happy and then immediately depressed," he said, giving her a small smile and turning his gaze out the window. "It's been a month since I've been here. Do I ever get a couple days off?"

"In the beginning, you'll get half days off," she said, "unless you overdo it or are recuperating from something. In that case, your team will shift your schedule."

He nodded and continued to stare outside.

She clipped her notebook together and placed her tablet down with such force that it had his head coming around. "You look depressed," she said. "Why don't we go outside and visit with the animals?"

His gaze went back to the window, where the early morning sun was dappling across the trees. He nodded. "I can get out there myself though," he said. "Go do your shift."

"I can do my shift if and when I want to," she said, her arms slowly crossing over her chest. She studied him for a long moment. "This isn't a pity request."

At that, he frowned. "I never thought that you were saying that out of pity," he said carefully. "That would be a really terrible thing."

"It would, wouldn't it?" she said cheerfully. "I just thought that maybe you would feel a little happier if you could get outside in the sunshine." She quickly whipped his wheelchair up to the side of his bed and said, "Come on. Let's go. We'll play hooky for an hour."

He grinned at her. "Only if it comes with coffee."

"That can be arranged," she said.

He still wasn't dressed—he was in his boxers as he slipped into the wheelchair.

She looked at him and said, "You'll be cold."

He snagged his T-shirt from the top of the dresser and some shorts, putting them on quickly, and then rolled his way to the hallway. "Are you coming?" he called back, laughing.

She grinned. He caught the bright twitch of her lips as

he went around the corner. That made him feel better. If he could make her feel better, maybe it would make him feel better. Then he realized that she was probably trying to make him feel better, and that would make her feel better too. He sighed, and it came out a little too heavy.

"No, none of that," she said.

"I just realized you didn't look like you had a good morning either," he said.

"Nope, I didn't," she said. "One patient who I have worked with for six months thought he was going home this week, and he found out last night he has to stay for another two weeks. He's pretty upset."

"I can imagine," Finn said with feeling. "It's hard enough being here, but, if your family's on the other side of the country and you're looking to go home, well ..."

"Exactly the problem with him," she said. "He's got two little girls and a wife. They've flown out once, but they don't have the money to keep making the trip."

"Ouch," he said. "That hurts. Kids grow up so fast, and six months is huge."

"So true," she said. "So he was very off this morning. I tried to cheer him up, but he'll take a little bit of time to get out of this funk."

"And, of course, his funk affects your funk."

At that, she laughed out loud. "Well, I wasn't in such a funk. I didn't sleep well last night."

"Why not?" he asked.

"I don't know," she said cheerfully. She spun his wheelchair with a backstep, turned him at the corner and said, "Let's go get coffee." Instead of going into the line, like he'd been heading, she wheeled him around to the far corner where the coffee service was, and there they stopped, picked up two hot cups of fresh brew, and she motioned him outside.

They went down a long ramp, and he said, "I've never even been in the pool yet."

"No," she said, "you don't get to go into the pool until the therapists say you're cleared for it."

"That's a bummer," he said as he studied the clean blue water. "It looks absolutely perfect right now."

"Talk to your therapist," she said. "Chances are you could go in now."

"It's supposed to be good for sore muscles, isn't it?"

She laughed. "It's not me you're trying to convince. Convince your therapist," she said. "I don't have the right to give you permission to go in there."

"Drat," he said amiably. "I'm talking to the wrong person."

"You are," she said. "Now, if the hot tub would calm you down and ease some of your back pain, then maybe, but that's not really your problem."

"Muscle knots," he said instantly. "It would help with the muscle knots."

She laughed. "Now, if you'd said that first, I'd have jumped on it immediately."

He was still carrying both cups of coffee as they went past the pool and patio area around to the back where there was a heavy gravel path. It went all the way around the building so that people could come for a walk, whether rolling along on wheelchairs or on crutches. Using whatever mobility they could, this was a space for them. "A lot of thought's gone into this place, hasn't it?"

"You have no idea," she said. "Dani and her father have done so much here."

"Speaking of which, where's the major?" he asked. "I saw him the first day across the room, and I haven't seen him since."

"He was at a conference," she said. "He should be back today."

"Good, I want to see him," he said. "I doubt he remembers me, but I certainly remember him."

"Was he already back from the war then?"

"Yes," Finn said, his voice dropping. "He was a very angry man with a lot of issues."

"Good, then you should see him now," she said. "He's completely different."

They stopped at the side where the horses dotted the fields on the hillside.

He asked, "How many does she have right now?"

"Hi," Dani said from off to one side, where he hadn't seen her. "Five, and I'm boarding four right now."

He grinned at her. "Aren't you a sight for sore eyes?" He looked and motioned at her jeans. "Have you been out riding or just communing with the horses?"

"Communing with the horses," she said, "and Lovely." She pointed out the small llama that was, as always, beside Appie. "She's such a beautiful addition to the place."

"But she will grow up," he warned her. "She'll grow up into a big spitting llama."

At that, Dani went off in peals of laughter. "And I'm okay with that too," she said warmly. "There's room for all of God's creatures."

"Even spiders?" he teased.

She nodded. "Even spiders." She looked at the coffee he was holding for him and Fiona. "Enjoy your early morning outing," she said. "I've got to have a shower and get ready for work." And she disappeared up the pasture.

He stared at the landscape until he noted a beautiful house up on the hillside. He glanced back at Fiona. "Is that Dani's place?"

"It is," she said. "Too many nights she doesn't even get that far. Lots of times you have to wake her up in her office and send her home because she's been working too hard."

"I think that's the problem when you have a business like this," he said. "A business which is a burning passion. She was always all about helping others."

"She still is," she said. "She met Aaron, her fiancé, here."

"I heard about that," he said. "I think Elliot mentioned it in one of his emails."

"Well, they're doing really well together," she said. "He's off in vet school. Like you, he was missing some body parts and wanted to find out what to do with his life."

"Yeah, that's another big thing. We all have funding from our time in the service. There's apparently a fair bit of it, if we want to go back to school and get new training, although I don't imagine all of it's covered," he said, "but certainly enough of it that most of us can get retrained as we need to."

"There are definitely some budgetary guidelines," she said. "We've come across it with a few of our patients. But most men have found a way to make it work."

"I haven't even thought about my future," he said. "For a long time, all I felt was that I had absolutely nothing to offer anymore. Feeling I couldn't work a job and, therefore, wasn't a man."

"And now?"

"Now I feel like there's got to be all kinds of things that I *could* do," he said. "I just don't know what I *want* to do."

"And that's a huge difference, isn't it?" she asked with a bright smile. She stepped in front of him, took one of the coffees from his hand, walked a few feet away to a large rock on the side of the pathway and sat down.

"Will you get in trouble for being here with me?" He frowned at the thought. He loved spending time with her but hated to think it'd cause her trouble.

She shook her head. "No, I was on duty early this morning anyway, and they don't clock-watch here, which is really good."

"They probably can't," he said. "It seems like you guys are always around."

"Because it's not just a job," she said. "Everyone becomes part of our family."

He nodded, instantly understanding what she meant. "That's good," he said. "That's the way it should be. That's the way it was in the military, and I guess I'm hoping to find something similar."

"Well, we had three friends who were here all at the same time, although most of them have left by now but have stayed close in town. I know that they were getting together and doing some things as a group," she said. "Building up that supportive brotherhood bond."

"But they probably already had that bond before they left the military, didn't they?"

She nodded. "I believe so. I think they were all part of the same team."

"Ouch," he said, "to have three injured to the extent that they have to be here means it was pretty ugly."

"I think that's a very mild word for it," she said with a half smile. "What kinds of things would you like to do?"

He looked at her in surprise. "Well, sometimes I think

about working with animals, and then I think I can't make a living doing that. Sometimes I think I should get back to my art, and then I talk myself out of that and think I can't do that anymore. I really have no idea. I do have an electrician's license," he said. "I did get a trade when I was in the military, but I'm not sure I want to do that anymore."

"You're an artist?"

Of course, she'd glommed onto that one. "I used to sketch," he said. "I don't know that I do anymore."

She studied both his hands and asked, "Were your arms affected?"

"No," he said, lifting his hands, wiggling his fingers around. "They're perfectly capable of drawing. It's just the disconnect between my mind and my heart. I used to sketch from my heart, and, right now, all I see are images of accidents and war. I used to see animals all the time. It's one of the connections that I had with Dani. She loved her horses, and I used to sketch her horses for her. All kinds of poses, sometimes cartoony. But I haven't done it for years now." He looked at his hands and said, "I don't even know if I still can."

Chapter 6

F IONA WOULD HAVE to talk to Dani about that, see just how talented Finn really was because maybe something was there that he could do as a full-time career. She'd seen people with little talent take off. She still didn't understand some of the more modernistic stuff, but it wasn't for her to judge. If Finn could do something that Dani would appreciate in terms of horses, then he was certainly in the right part of the country for it. "I don't know about a full-time living," she said quietly, "but art can certainly be a huge passion and an outlet for healing."

His lips quirked. "You see? That's how I always know that you're in the right field," he said. "Even when you're not at work, you're at work."

She chuckled at that. "Just because artwork is great for the soul and helps you to heal and all kinds of things," she said, "that doesn't mean that I'm on duty." She looked at her watch and sighed. "But it does mean I have to get back on duty pretty soon."

He looked at his empty cup and then at her and smiled. "Thanks for this," he said. "It really did help."

"Good," she said, standing. "Let's take the long way around. I could use a little bit more exercise."

"Don't you swim in the pool?"

"I do," she said. "Definitely I do. Just haven't been in

since I've gotten back from vacation. But I should. Just doing a few laps helps me let go of my day."

"What about horseback riding?"

"Not my thing," she said. "I wouldn't mind running alongside them, but I can't say that I particularly want to ride them."

"Do you jog?"

"Again I used to," she said, "but somehow it seems to have been something I let slip away. But I do love it," she said thoughtfully. "Maybe that is something I should get back into."

"You've got beautiful trails here to jog."

"There're trails all across the property," she said. "It's one of the reasons I got into running. There was so much to see, and it is just such a beautiful geographical region to step out and get exercise and breathe fresh air and enjoy my surroundings," she said. "But time is like that. It gets away from you, and you stop doing something one day. The next thing you know, it's been a week or two, and you're way behind."

"Agreed," he said. "That's like my artwork."

"Well, I tell you what. I'll start jogging again if you start drawing again."

He laughed. "I don't have any supplies here. You just need runners, and then you can go."

"Well," she said as she pushed him around the pathway, "I'll check around to see what we have hidden away and see what we might come up with."

"Well, if you can," he said doubtfully, "and to keep you exercising and in good health, I agree."

She was still laughing about his comment when her shift was over, but he'd kept her smiling all day, and it hadn't been a terribly easy day either. When she walked out to the front reception area at the end of her shift, she talked to Mandy and asked, "Hey, do we have any art supplies here?"

Mandy, harried and in the middle of answering multiple phone calls, looked up at her and said, "Talk to Dani."

Fiona stepped off to the side and saw Dani sitting in her office, her feet on the desk and the phone to her ear, and figured it probably wasn't the right time. Fiona walked down the hallway to the supply room and stood staring at the items in front of her, but she didn't know what Finn might need.

"Fiona, did you need me?" Dani called out to her.

She retraced her steps to Dani's office and saw she was done with her call. "Hey, I didn't want to disturb you," she said. "I was just looking for something."

"What is it you need?"

Fiona plunked herself down on the chair across from Dani and said, "Something I'm trying to get Finn back to doing," she said, so she told Dani about their deal.

At that, Dani's face brightened. "You have no idea how talented he is," she exclaimed. "I mean, like seriously talented. He could be doing this as a full-time career."

"Well, he's looking for some idea of what to do with his life but says that he's not even sure he can draw anymore."

Dani walked around and closed the door, then pointed out a sketch of wild horses racing across rough terrain. "He did that in about ten minutes flat."

Fiona gasped. She stood and stared. "That's Finn's work?"

Dani stood beside her and nodded. "It so is. I was having a really crappy day back then, and I had these pieces of paper I was supposed to be doing summary reports on. Anyway, he snatched one of my pages and made me really mad. Well, I sat here, having a cup of coffee, trying to calm down. When he lifted up the sketch, I could just feel all the pain and anguish and frustration drain away. He's that talented. Just look at the detail."

Fiona couldn't stop staring. Five horses streamed across the field, but he'd done it with minimum strokes. The detail was there, and yet, it wasn't the whole of the picture. It was just marvelous. "It's like they're part of the wind," she whispered.

"That's exactly it," Dani said with a heartfelt sigh. "So, anything to get Finn back to drawing is money I'm quite happy to spend."

"I don't know what he needs though," she said. "He seemed to think that we wouldn't have any supplies here, and I don't think he's looking for just a couple pieces of printer paper."

"No, we need sketchbooks for him. I think we have an excursion going into town Thursday," she said, reaching for her calendar. "Maybe I'll run in myself."

"Can you spare the time?" Fiona asked, puzzled. Normally Dani didn't do personal trips like this.

Dani flashed her a smile. "For Finn? To get him back to his art? Absolutely."

Fiona was delighted that she'd brought it up. "I may have to go get new running shoes then too because the other half of the deal is that I start jogging again," she said with a laugh. "It's something that I used to always love, but somehow, like so many things in life, it fell away, along with the rest of my schedule."

Dani nodded solemnly. "Which is why I was out there this morning, just to trample around with the horses. I want to get back to riding on a more regular basis too, but, like you and the jogging, and Finn and the drawing, it's something you have to work at to keep in your life. And it makes no sense because it's what brings us joy. Yet so many other things we label as priorities, and the things that bring us pure joy end up not even making the list."

Fiona was still thinking about Dani's words as she walked back to her on-site rooms. Like many of the other staff here, she had a small apartment to herself. She didn't have a kitchenette because she didn't need it. She had all the food she could want at Hathaway House. And anytime she wanted a special meal, she already knew the chefs personally, and they were more than happy to accommodate her. It was easy to live here. It was easy to enjoy the food at the cafeteria. It was easy to accept the lifestyle and let everything else slide.

She did her job—usually more than the thirty-five hours a week she was paid for—but again that's because they were family.

But she hadn't gone in the pool lately. She hadn't gone for her walks. She hadn't gone for her runs. And she didn't have any friends in town anymore. For a while, she used to meet up with a group for lunch every once in a while and catch a movie, but now it seemed they'd all gone their different directions.

She checked her watch and realized that dinner was about to start pretty soon. She either wanted to go early or wanted to go late to miss the rush. So today she would go late. She walked back to her place, quickly switched out of her uniform and had a hot shower. There, with her hair freshly braided, noticing the length and realizing a haircut was something else she needed to do, she dressed in a soft cotton dress that flowed around her legs. It helped the patients to see her out of uniform, how she was a normal person, not just a staff member. Ready for her dinner, she stepped out of her place, closed the door behind her and saw Stan standing off to one side, staring up the hills. She walked over to him. "Wow, don't you look like you're lost."

He gave her a half-smile, but it was a teary smile.

"I'm sorry. I guess you lost somebody today."

He nodded slowly. "Yes, I did. I tried hard, but I couldn't make it happen." He gave half a whistle, and Helga, the great big three-legged Newfoundlander dog, came racing toward them. Fiona bent down and gave her a big cuddle. "You keeping them close? I don't think Finn has even met these guys."

"Well, Racer's pretty well hard to track down at any one given time in the day," he said. "Helga here had a little bit of trouble with her back legs, so I've mostly kept her downstairs where I can keep an eye on her."

"Is she okay now?" she asked in concern.

Stan reached down and affectionately scratched her long back. "She is. Now if we could stop everybody from feeding her," he said, "she'd do much better."

"She looks like a big girl, but I hardly think she needs to go on a diet."

"No, she probably doesn't, but too much human food isn't good for her either."

"At least most of the residents here know not to feed Chickie," she said with a laugh.

"Well, the repercussions on that one are pretty instantaneous," he said. "One guy fed him when you were gone. Poor Chickie chucked almost immediately all over him. He didn't try it again after that."

"Serves him right," she said. "These animals have already got enough physical problems. The reason they live as long as they do is because we follow strict rules with them."

"It's not like Chickie's getting any exercise either," he said with a smile. "Everybody carries that poor little dog around."

"Well, I don't think Helga has the same issue. She's too big to carry," she said.

Helga lifted her head and woofed at her.

She reached down, patted her gently and asked Stan, "Are you coming up for dinner?"

Stan stuffed his hands in his pockets and nodded. "Yes, I should." He looked at her, smiled and said, "You're looking very pretty tonight."

"Just one of the things that I was thinking about today," she said as they walked slowly toward the cafeteria. "Living here becomes too hard to separate our private lives from work. How often do we not bother getting changed out of our scrubs? We stick around, have dinner in our work clothes and then go home and change." She shook her head. "I should be going home, getting changed so that I feel like my workday ends and that I have a personal life again."

"It's part of that whole syndrome of living here, isn't it?" he asked. "You try to separate it, but it doesn't really happen."

"True enough," she said. "Are you sitting with anybody for dinner?"

"With you, if you'll let me," he said, holding her arm.

She chuckled, tucked her hand in the crook of his elbow and said, "I'd be pleased. Thank you very much, sir."

"You should be dating some of these young bucks, not hanging around with an oldie, like me."

"I think you're a whole ten years older than I am," she joked. "You're just having a rough day."

"Some days are like that," he admitted.

"On the other hand," she said with a smile, "Lovely looks lovely."

He burst out laughing. "Can you imagine someone named her that?"

"Can you imagine keeping her named like that?" she teased.

He just rolled his eyes at her. "As far as Dani is concerned, it's a *lovely* name."

Fiona chuckled. They made their way to where the plates were stacked to see Dennis waiting for them. She said, "You're another one who never seems to leave his job."

Dennis's face split, his white teeth flashing in a huge grin, and he said, "Nope, this is where I belong."

"Hardly," she said, "but I've never seen you sitting down and eating out here."

"That's because we have lots of tables in the back," he said. "We're a big family back here too, so we like to sit together."

"As long as you don't feel like you're not allowed to sit out here, that you can't sit out here or that you're not welcome to sit out here," she said.

"Nope, that's the last thing we feel," he said. "Now, what will you have for dinner?"

She looked down and said, "Chicken pot pies. Are they homemade?"

"Is today Sunday?" he asked with a teasing grin. "Of course they're homemade. I made them myself."

"In that case, I want one," she said, "and a big salad."

"You've got to eat something besides salad," he said.

"Oh, I will," she said with a big grin. "I fully intend to eat a slice of apple pie with it."

FIVE DAYS LATER, Finn found himself crippled with cramps again. Fiona had brought Chickie with her to stop by his room, but the tiny dog was staying because he wanted to.

Finn's heart broke when he thought about how small this little dog was, curled up against his chest like he was home. "How old is Chickie?"

"I have forgotten, actually," she said. "I think he's four or five. Stan has done a lot to keep him alive and thriving. But we have a very strict rule about not feeding him because the wrong food will upset his stomach immediately."

"Which is just another problem along with his back legs," he said.

"Right. But he is a well-loved mascot," she said as she worked Finn's leg.

At one particular spot, he gasped and rolled his face into the pillow, feeling the pain shuddering up and down his back.

She whispered, "Sorry. It's really not wanting to loosen up." Finally, she stopped, and she said, "You're in your boxers. How about we get you into a bathing suit and get you to the hot tub. I can keep working on it down there."

He rolled over, gasping. "Just the thought of getting into the hot tub ..."

"Not a problem. I'll help you," she said. She walked over to his chest of drawers, pulled out a pair of swim trunks and held them out. He nodded, reaching for them. She walked over and snagged the wheelchair, came back and said, "Do you need help getting changed?"

"Nope. I'm done," he said, throwing off the covers and picking up Chickie again.

She helped him, half-lifting, half-sliding him into the wheelchair. And, with him still hanging on to little Chickie in his arms, she quickly wheeled him down the hallway. But she didn't go the normal way. He was surprised to find himself inside an elevator. He looked up at her. "I didn't even know you could go this way."

"Normally we can't," she said, "but this time I think it's necessary."

"Good," he said, "the faster, the better."

Before the doors even opened, he realized he was already at the pool level and close to it. She walked up to the nearby hot tub, parked the wheelchair, put on the brakes, lifted the little dog from his lap and put him on a pile of towels at the side. Chickie hopped off immediately, running to the edge of the water at the pool.

Fiona said, "Now, slowly, I want you to get up and get into this warm water." She helped him up the hot tub steps and then, stumbling, half-falling, he let himself collapse into the hot tub. He groaned as the warm water eased up over his body and splashed his face. He let himself sink to the bottom for a moment before coming up slowly to get a breath. He opened his eyes to see her staring at him.

"Glad you came up when you did," she said. "I did not want to have to go in after you, fully dressed."

He smiled and asked, "Can you come in?"

"I can if I need to," she said, "and, if we keep working those legs, I might have to." She glanced around and said, "But I can't leave you alone."

He looked at her in surprise.

She said, "There are rules."

Just then a big male walked over. He looked at Finn, smiled and said, "I'm Shane. I'll stand watch, if you want,

Fiona. Actually, I'm already dressed for the water, if you want me to go to work on those legs." He took a couple steps, already in a bathing suit, sat down on the edge of the hot tub and said, "I could see from the way you went in how your legs are all twisted up in pain."

Finn nodded, gasping. "I guess therapy was too much."

"Well, I'm a therapist too," Shane said, scolding him. "You have to tell your therapist this. Otherwise, there's no way for us to know. We can adjust your treatments."

"I've already told him that," Fiona said from the side. She watched as Shane carefully worked on Finn's legs. She nodded, seeing some of the tight lines on Finn's face relax, and asked, "You okay?"

He nodded, gasping, and said, "I will be now. This water's heaven-sent."

"It's perfect for this," Shane said. He carefully worked out the knots; then he looked over at Fiona and said, "We're good here. I'll get him back up to his room."

Finn lifted a hand, waved at her and said, "Thanks." He watched as she walked away. When he could, he sighed deeply and tried to shift his position, feeling the pain once again jarring his back. "It's my back and my legs," he whispered.

"Yep," Shane said. "We don't get simple injuries here. And everything is connected. People tend to forget that."

"I think it's my fault," Finn said. "I was pretty eager to get through my therapy today, and I pushed it."

"*Pushing it* to a certain extent is what we want. But *overdoing it* is the opposite of what we want."

"It's a fine line though," Finn said. And then, to his embarrassment, he felt and remembered his colostomy bag. "Oh, no." He reached down and said, "I don't think this is

73

supposed to get wet."

Shane looked at it, shrugged and said, "Why not? Everybody else does."

Finn felt the shock run through him. "Everyone else?"

"I think we've got six guys here with them right now," he said. "A couple are permanent. Others are waiting for their guts to heal until they can have surgery to fix things permanently. They are what they are." He was completely casual about it all.

As this was the first time Finn had been in water since he'd had the colostomy, Finn stared at the bag laying against his skin and said, "It's pretty ugly."

Shane looked up at him in surprise. "Not really," he said. "It's pretty normal. There are different bags you can get. Ones that aren't quite so big, ones that aren't quite so obvious maybe," he said, "but honestly, it's a miracle."

"Everybody keeps saying that," Finn said, "but it still seems like quite an eyesore. And, for anybody who's not used to it, it's pretty embarrassing."

Shane grinned at him. "You mean, it's embarrassing for you. Nobody here'll care. They've all got their own problems, missing pieces and body parts that have been redirected. That"—he nodded toward the colostomy bag—"that's nothing."

Relaxing, Finn sank back and said, "Yeah, but I wonder if the women think so."

"My buddy is married, and he's got one," Shane said with a laugh. "I don't think he gave a damn, and I know his wife sure as heck doesn't."

Finn loved to hear that. "I think, when you get to that stage, you're probably okay," he said, "but I imagine accidents are pretty embarrassing."

"Accidents can happen no matter where your feces exit your body," he said. "Sure, to you it's not sexy, but that doesn't mean that a woman will look at it the same way."

Finn didn't want to keep thinking about it. "The stump is bad enough," he said.

"Around here it's not like you even got a war wound if you don't have a stump," Shane said with a laugh. He started to rub long, lean strokes up and down the rippled muscles of Finn's leg. "See if you can stretch that out a little bit now."

Finn gently extended his leg, waiting for the pain to surface. But, when fully extended and his toes pointed, expecting it every second, he realized no cramp waited around the corner.

"Wow," Shane said. "That is so much better. Let's get the other one into the same shape. You can't have just one leg massaged. Gotta do the other one too."

"Well, the other one doesn't cramp," he said, shifting so he could get out the leg that had the stump. "I don't know why."

"Because it's not connected at the other end," Shane said, chuckling. "The leg that cramps, the tendons and muscles have connections at both sides. Here, they're damaged at the one end, so it won't cramp the same way. But that doesn't mean that they cannot be stiff and sore." He gently dug his fingers in, working the muscle all along the length, trying to ease up some of the stress. "And part of the problem is because that leg's tense, you tighten up on the good leg to compensate."

"I guess," he said. "I never thought of it that way."

"Your body is a fantastic machine," Shane said, "and it will do what it needs to do. The trouble is, if we interfere, we get emotions that make us react, and, as soon as we do that, the body has to compensate. It's a fine-tuned machine, and, as soon as it gets out of tune, then things have to happen in order to get it back to being a well-maintained body again."

"Got it," Finn said with a smile. "It's amazing just how much more normal that feels now." He shifted his other leg and then extended his leg at the knee. "Wow, I hadn't realized just how bad that cramp was."

"Who's your therapist?"

"Nicole," he said, "but it's not her fault."

"Well, it is, and it isn't," Shane said. "I'll have a talk with her."

"I don't want to get her in trouble," Finn argued.

"But, if you don't tell her the kind of aftereffects you're having," Shane said, "you're the one who's in trouble."

As it was, they didn't have to tell Nicole anything. She walked along the pool on the other side and saw Finn in the hot tub. She came racing over as her gaze went to Shane massaging the one leg. "Finn, are you okay?" She crouched at the hot tub.

Shane quickly explained. She shook her head. "You should have told me," she scolded.

"So everybody keeps telling me," Finn said with a half a smile. "I figured I was doing fine. Didn't realize that the cramps were something I was supposed to let you know about."

"Has it happened before?"

"Yes, every day."

There was a moment of silence, and then she just swore at him. Very gently, very politely, she said, "You have to tell me these things."

He waved a hand at her. "Consider yourself told," he said. "I gather the therapy is too much, and I'm weaker than

I thought."

"No," she said, "that's not it at all. It has to do entirely with the exercises we do, and that's something I need to know."

He nodded and smiled.

"I'll get you a drink and some relaxants to help those muscles," she said. "I'll be back in a minute."

"Make it a whiskey," he called out.

She laughed and said, "In your dreams."

He grinned and said to Shane, "One of the nice things about being here is the casualness of it all. The fact that I can tease her and sit here in a hot tub like this, it's huge."

"It is," Shane said. "I've been here for years, and I can't say there's any other place I'd want to work."

"You're lucky," he said, closing his eyes. "I don't know what I want to do anymore."

"But you're the artist, aren't you?"

Finn's gaze popped open. "I don't know who told you that," he said. "I used to dabble, but I don't know that I'm any good at it. And I haven't done it for years, so I'm sure that I'm beyond rusty."

"Uh-huh." Shane didn't say anything more but started working on a different muscle path that had Finn crying out. "Yeah," Shane said, "I'll ease up, but these knots need working out. You'll feel the next one since we're getting closer to the knee."

He kept working while Finn twisted in reaction. When he could, he gasped. "How come it's okay for you to hurt me, but it's not okay for the cramps themselves to hurt me?"

Shane laughed. "Because I know what I'm doing. The cramps are a reaction to the previous work. You won't get cramps from this. I'm taking the cramps away. Besides, no matter how odd this feels, I'm not really hurting you."

"I didn't know I had knots in there," he gasped out, grabbing his knee as Shane worked lightly right up against the bone.

Finally, Shane was done. He shifted back slightly and said, "Now kick your legs out as if you're swimming."

Finn tried to kick and was surprised to find how fluidly his legs moved. He stared at them in surprise. "Wow, that's amazing."

"Your structural integrity is compromised too," Shane said with a frown. "Has anybody worked on that?"

"I don't even know what you're talking about, so I'll say *no*," he said.

"In that case, we book you for it too," Shane said. He stepped up, held out his hand and said, "I want you to stand normally."

So, in the middle of the hot tub on his one good leg, he stood. But because they were in the water, it wasn't an effort to balance.

Shane said, "Now close your eyes and just stand, relaxed."

Finn did feel a little odd, but Shane walked around him several times and said, "Open your eyes now."

Finn did.

"Now I want you to try to take a step forward."

"You mean, a hop?"

"Yes and no," he said. "Imagine that you had your foot there, and I want you to take a step and then quickly take another step. Because you're in water you should be okay."

He did as he was instructed.

"Okay, now raise your arms out to the side." And with Finn's arms up parallel, Shane once again walked around him and took a look. "I want you to sit here and rest a bit," he said. "I'll grab a tablet so I can take some notes, and I'll take some photos too."

Finn looked at him in surprise. "Photos while I'm sitting here?"

"Yes, but then we'll do some more when you're standing upright. And I'll show you how you're compensating."

"Well, of course, I have to compensate," he said. "I'm missing my lower leg, for crying out loud."

"Yep, you sure are," Shane said. "But you're compensating for a whole lot more, so hang on. I'll show you in a minute."

Chapter 7

FIONA WALKED AWAY, determined to check on the men later. But she had other rounds to do—plus medications to sort, shipments to open up and inventory to mark off. While she stood here with a clipboard in her hand, going over the medications and checking them against her digital database, Dani came in. Fiona looked up and smiled.

Dani held up a large sketchbook and another smaller one.

"Oh, wow, are those for Finn?"

"They so are," Dani said. "I also picked up a case of pencils for him."

"A case?" she asked cautiously. "Not one?"

"I remember Finn having favorites," she said, "something about not all pencils being equal when it comes to sketching."

"Well, I don't sketch and don't know anyone who does," Fiona said, "so I bow to your expertise. Maybe we can deliver these to him later. I left him in Shane's care. He was having a lot of muscle knots so we got him to the hot tub."

"Oh, good," Dani said. "That hot tub has come in handy for a lot of people."

"Isn't that the truth. And, if we know Shane at all, he'll be all over Finn for his *structural integrity*."

"Right, Shane just came back from his latest course, and,

if he can help at all, then I'm sure Finn wouldn't mind."

"I'm sure it's more than a case of *wouldn't mind*," Fiona said. "I think Finn is eager to do whatever needs to be done, and that's probably how he ended up in trouble in the first place. A little too anxious, a little too eager, and working a little too hard, without letting people know where he stood."

"That's common here," Dani said. "Way too common."

"Right? Anyway, if you want, you can give him the art supplies," Fiona said.

Dani shook her head. "No, I think you should." She turned and walked out again.

Fiona waited until the end of her shift because she still had lots of work to do, and, even then, she didn't get it all done. She signed off after her shift, consulting with her replacement over a couple files.

As she stood to leave, she smiled and said, "I have one delivery to make." She picked up the sketchbooks and the pencils and walked out. She had no idea how Finn would take this and wasn't sure if she should say it was from Dani or not but figured it couldn't hurt. Fiona didn't know if, at this point, he'd get angry or be happy about it. She knocked on his closed door but got no answer. She frowned and walked to the cafeteria to see if he was there and then headed over to the railing, where she could study the pool and the hot tub below to see if maybe Finn just hadn't made it back to his room yet. Shane was there, but he was working with a different patient. She called out to him. "How's Finn doing?"

"He's fine," he said. "He went to have a shower and a nap."

She nodded and realized he was likely still asleep. She didn't want to disturb him, but he might be just resting at this point. At his door, she tapped again ever-so-lightly and listened, but still, she heard no answer. She carried the sketchbooks back to her place, dropped them on the couch and then went for a quick shower and a change herself.

He'd be awake for dinner so she could see him then. She dressed up particularly nicely in a dress again and braided her hair and then stepped outside to visit with the beautiful little Lovely. She gently stroked the llama's soft ears, loving the trusting soul so eager for affection. Appie was a little more distant but came over anyway. Fiona didn't have any treats for them, and she definitely didn't have any feed for them.

She wondered who looked after that, but nobody was around to ask. She could ask Stan, but that would mean going back inside, and that almost felt like work. Instead, she went for a long walk in the pasture as Appie and Lovely walked beside her. It was so nice to be outside to enjoy the green grass and the sunshine. She sat on a large rock, perfect for sitting, and enjoyed the beautiful view. It was really a special location.

She should have brought a cup of coffee with her, something to help her relax and destress from her day. Today wasn't that bad; it was just work, and sometimes work was, … well, work.

Inventory was always irritating because she kept missing bottles and then would find them in places where people hadn't put them back. And, of course, as soon as medications went missing, alarm bells went off. Missing medication was something they had to keep a strict eye on. Of course, all the medicine cabinets were locked, but she knew perfectly well that many of the men in her care could unlock it easily. These patients came with such a varied set of skills that the staff made sure to keep track of medications a little closely than they might at another location, and there would always be at least one difficult patient.

Thankfully it wasn't Finn. Although she was pretty sad to see the way his body had reacted to the physical therapy, with Shane on it now, she knew that Finn's assigned therapist, Nicole, would have her methods questioned, and Finn's medical team would have further consultations to make sure that Finn wasn't going through unnecessary pain. A certain amount of pain in order to push through limits and break through barriers was one thing, but pain afterward to the point of cramping up and down his legs and his back was something else. He should have been given medication to help relax the muscles too. Then again Finn was stubborn and might have refused. She heard a voice and looked out across the field to see somebody in a wheelchair waving up at her. She waved back at Finn.

She hopped off her rock and walked slowly down the hill, the animals once again following her. As she got to the fence, she smiled at him. "What are you doing?"

"Did you knock on my door?" he asked. "I thought I heard somebody, and I came and checked and kept on going until I was already up and outside. I saw you in the field here when I was grabbing a cup of coffee," he said, "and it looked too nice to leave you alone." He apologized, saying, "I'm sorry if you wanted the alone time though."

She smiled, shook her head and said, "Time with you is always welcome."

"I hope you mean that," he said. "It's hard enough being in a place like this, but, when you find somebody you truly connect with, that makes it very special. But it's easy to overstep the bounds and misunderstand what that relationship truly is."

That stopped her for a moment. She tilted her head to the side and asked, "Do you need to analyze it?" She could see him hesitate, and she nodded. "You do."

She sat on the top of the fence, stared down at him and said, "The least you could have done was brought a second coffee," she complained good-naturedly.

"True," he said. "I could have. Didn't think of it. I'm sorry."

"Don't be." She waited a second and then said, "And I can tell that you're avoiding the conversation."

He nodded. "So I guess that's my answer."

"Nope," she said, "it isn't your answer. You surprised me, but I shouldn't have been surprised because I could see something was between us, but again I have to be a little more careful, being a nurse. I mean, I'm your medical caregiver. One of many, true, but it's something that we're always much more aware of."

"Are relationships not allowed here?" he asked lightly.

"Well, if that were the case, a lot of people would be in trouble," she said, chuckling. "And Dani started it anyway. Aaron was one of the patients here."

"Right," he said. "I guess in my mind I hadn't put that two and two together, but, of course, if she says it's okay ..."

"It's frowned on in most centers just because it's easy to misunderstand the boundaries of where patient medical care stops and gratitude, emotional dependency starts with a personal relationship."

"Got it," he said.

"However, on my side," she said, "I'm quite happy to see you after work hours."

"Which is right now, correct?"

"Absolutely," she said. "Besides, I have a present for

you."

That stopped him for a moment. "I can't remember the last time I had a present," he said, in surprise.

"Well, it's from both me and Dani," she said. "Come on. We can go to my place, and I'll give it to you."

"If I can roll over to your place," he said, "that would be fine. I'm still dealing with the aftereffects of all the cramping earlier."

"Did you take the muscle relaxants I left on your night table?"

"I found them, yes, thanks. And the note."

"If you need more, tell me," she said. "Plus, I'm sure some changes will be made to your PT schedule after this."

"Well, there'll definitely be some changes on the exercises," he said. "I'm not sure how much value any of this is doing to my back, as it seems like we help one body part and the next part screams."

"And I think that's what Shane was talking about regarding your structural integrity," she said. "Because, if your skeleton itself isn't standing straight, everything else is working to compensate. In your case, because you're missing so many back muscles and you're missing part of a leg, all along your right side, then your body is forced to compensate a lot. Shane will likely add in some extra stuff for you."

"My schedule is pretty booked as it is," he said with a bit of life in his voice. "It's hard to find time for anything else in the day."

"This is your job right now," she said, her voice serious. "Everything to do with you and your health is your job *and* your hobby."

"Got it. But afterward," he said, "when therapy's over, it's nice to step away and to spend some time outside, forgetting that this is why I'm here."

"Absolutely," she said. "And, if we get to do it with a friend, it's even better." She smiled and tousled his hair. When he laughed, she stepped away and said, "Come on, this way." And she picked up the pace. She knew he was forced to wheel a little faster, but she wouldn't totally compensate for his injuries. Once you started doing that, there was no end to it.

At her place, she left the door open so he could wheel in, and she walked to the couch, picked up the art supplies and turned around. His gaze went to the sketchbooks, and his eyebrows shot up.

"I know you don't think you can draw anymore, but sometimes in the evening, sometimes in the morning, maybe when you just want something different to do," she said, "I think it might be good for your soul if you try it again. Besides, we made a deal." She held out the two sketchbooks.

He took them slowly. "You know what? There's something very special about having a clean page in front of you." He opened the big pad, pulling the cover piece back and folding it under his hands, gently stroking across the slightly rough surface. "And this paper is perfect."

"Is there a difference in paper?" she asked curiously.

"A lot of difference," he said. "I'll have to find some pencils."

Immediately she held out the case that she had in her hand.

He looked at it, smiled and asked, "Dani is behind this, isn't she?"

"I was behind it, and then Dani went to town, brought everything, and I'm delivering. According to Dani, pencils aren't created equal either," she said.

"No," he said, "they definitely aren't." He opened the box and shook a few out into his hand. He smiled and said, "This is the best thing anybody could have gotten me. I don't guarantee to create anything worth keeping, and I certainly am not promising any finished prints," he said, "but it would be nice to see what my fingers can create. Just maybe doodle a little bit."

"And that's all that's asked of you," she said. "They're gifts. They don't come with strings."

"And that's the best kind of gift," he said.

"It's the only kind of gift," she said. "Everything else then becomes a barter. So, why don't we take this back to your room, and then we can go get dinner together."

"Is that like a date?" he teased, waggling his eyebrows.

She chuckled. "Absolutely," she said, "as much of a date as we can have, considering we both live here."

"But it's about making every day and every meeting special," he said. "Dates don't have to be anything more than a cup of coffee in a field. It's just an appointed time to spend our moments together."

"I like that," she said, thinking about it. "It's a nice definition. And, in that case, yes," she said. "This is definitely a date. We get to have a meal together where we can talk."

"Good," he said, "but please, not about muscle cramps anymore. I'm so over those."

After stopping by his room, she headed into the cafeteria with him at her side, laughing cheerfully. "At least you have a sense of humor," she said smiling.

"I do have that," he said. "And honestly, I've needed it."

FINN WENT TO bed with a smile on his face and woke up in the middle of the night, almost screaming in agony. He tried to stifle his cries, but it was hard. Very quickly, muted lights were turned on as people came running in. He tried to tell them he was okay, but he could only gasp in pain. It was his back, not his legs this time, as his back muscles were coming alive and were working harder than they ever had before.

Now they screamed with pain and cramped from an overwhelming amount of built-up acid. He lay here, desperately trying not to bawl as warm hands laid hot cloths on his back, trying to calm the agonizing muscle spasms. That eased the immediate pain. Hands coated in cream gently massaged the insertion point of each of the muscle bands, then smoothed down their lengths, trying to relax the knots.

Finally, when he could, he gasped out, "Thank you."

"Do you want anything for the pain?" a woman asked.

He twisted his head. "Fiona, is that you?"

"Yes," she said, "I'm doing a nightshift to help out a friend."

"Lucky you," he said. And then he groaned as she worked on one muscle deep in his back.

"Yes," she said, "lucky me." She gently worked his back muscles, her tone even and calm, as she helped reduce the stress on his system until finally, he could straighten again, and he rolled over onto his back.

"This isn't exactly how I would want my night to be with you," he said.

"Me either," she said cheerfully. "We had dinner and a lovely evening, and now you're having a rough night. Did you expect me not to come help?"

"I just wish there wasn't the need for it," he said softly.

In all honesty, the sheet was soaked underneath him too, but he wouldn't mention that to her. Finally, she gently stretched out his calves, pulling them up tight against his chest and doing several exercises to try to relax the rest of his body that had tensed with the initial shocking pain. After he'd done those, he lay here, shaking, but it was mostly a slight tremor now. He whispered, "That's much better, thank you."

"No problem," she said. "Now I'll get you to sit in your wheelchair, and I'll quickly change your bedding."

"No," he said, embarrassed. "Just leave it."

"Of course, I'm not leaving it," she said. "Come on. Get up and into the chair with you." He sat up and then realized that he hadn't made any attempt to hide his colostomy bag. He stared down at it suddenly, but his silence had already alerted her. She looked at it and smiled and said, "Prissy, one of the nurses here, has purple and pink polka-dot bags."

He looked at her in surprise. "One of the staff has one of these?"

"Of course," she said. "Why wouldn't they? Depending on the health issues, this is a hell of an answer." She helped him gently sit in the chair.

He said, "It's located in an odd space. My belt fits underneath it, but I want it to be below that."

"Then your pants won't fit," she said. "I think they put it where it worked the best for your particular issues."

"I know," he said. "It's just ..." And his voice petered out.

"You're worrying too much," she said, "but I can get you a hot pink and purple one, if you'd rather."

At that, he burst out laughing. "That'll dent my manhood even more," he said.

She stopped, walked around in front of him and said, "You're not really afraid that that colostomy bag will affect how women view you, are you?" Her ominous tone made him realize she took offense on behalf of all womankind.

"I don't know how women will take it," he said carefully, trying to explain. "I can only tell you how I'm taking it, and, to me, it's an eyesore. It's an embarrassment, and it's something I would prefer not to show anybody."

"Well, it's a good thing that your date tonight was with me, and I've already seen that," she said blithely as she went over to the bed, seemingly now completely unconcerned with his words as she stripped off the bedsheets. She quickly removed the pillowcases as well and, within minutes, had his bed made up for him with crisp clean linens. She took the others out to the hallway and tossed them somewhere that he couldn't see. When she returned, she asked, "Now can you sleep? Would you like something else, like a hot cup of tea?"

"Actually," he said, "that's not a half-bad idea." He got up and made his way awkwardly with his crutches to the bathroom, and, when he was done and came back out again, he felt better but now more awake. "Can't wait to get a prosthetic on this stump again," he said.

"You had one before, didn't you?" she asked, pulling back the sheets and the blankets so he could get into bed. As soon as he lay down, she pulled the covers up to his waist.

"I did," he said, "but I kept soring up, and then I got an infection from it. So they changed something on the skin flaps to give me a little bit more cushion and did something to one of the veins that was too close to the surface."

"So it was a relatively minor surgery, but hopefully one that, once it's healed, will make a major difference," she said.

He looked up at her. "I like the way you think," he said.

"It was minor surgery, but, of course, no surgery is minor."

"Exactly," she said. "If you're okay now"—she switched on his bedside lamp, then walked over to turn off the overhead light—"I'll put the teakettle on. Then I'll do rounds and will bring you a hot cup of something. A Sleepytime chamomile or a hot lemon. What would you like?"

"One of my favorites, honestly," he said, "is a hot lemon. But only half the honey."

"You got it," she said. "Have you got a book to read or something?"

He nodded. "I'll be fine. I've got my phone, and I'll surf the web."

"Back in a few minutes then," she said, and, just like that, she was gone.

He lay in bed and thought about her reaction to his colostomy and then her comment about having seen it before. And, of course, she had. He hadn't even thought anything of it because she was a nurse. She'd seen things like this all the time. But, as a girlfriend, or a potential one, it was different. Or he thought it would be. Did that make her one-in-a-million because it didn't bother her? Or did that just make him an idiot for thinking it would bother everyone? Sure, a lot of women wouldn't like it. A lot of women would be turned off by it, but, just because a lot of women were, didn't mean that every woman would be.

Chapter 8

FIONA QUICKLY FINISHED her rounds, made him a cup of tea and stopped back in his room. She half expected him to be asleep again, but instead, he lay here, staring through his window at the dark night, his cell phone on his waist, his eyes open as if deep in thought.

"Penny?"

His lips twitched. He rolled over, smiled at her and said, "It's worth a dollar at least."

"Watch it," she teased. "I have a dollar in my wallet."

His smile widened. "You're a really nice person, you know that?"

"That's usually a brush-off," she said. She could see the surprise in his eyes. "It's what you tell somebody when you don't want to go out with them. *You're really nice, but ...*"

"Except for one thing," he said. "I never said *but.*"

"That's true," she said with a smile. "Is that because I didn't give you a chance?"

"You're a really nice person, *and* I like you a lot," he said firmly.

She laughed at that. "Well, in that case, I think you're a very nice person. I like you too."

"See? Now we've already said that we like each other, and we've already had our first date, and we've already met at midnight to do all kinds of things to my body," he said with a snicker, "so what's next in our unique relationship?"

She shook her head. "Not sure there's any preset one-size-fits-all pathway when it comes to relationships."

"You're sure you're allowed to have them here?" he asked, no longer teasing.

"Of course," she said. "As long as there's no hanky-panky," she added with a twinkle in her eye, "because that's definitely not allowed here."

"Of course not," he said, "that would cause all kinds of chaos because everybody'll want some for themselves."

At that, she laughed. "Well, we're not exactly a brothel," she said, "and we don't accommodate families or partners. So it's definitely not that type of a home."

"Understood," he said, "but you can't blame a guy for thinking."

"Not at all," she said. She headed toward his sketchbooks and pencils. "If you can't go to sleep right now, why don't you do some sketching?"

It was almost like a switch turned off in him. He nodded slowly and said, "I think I'm tired."

She took that as her permission to leave. "Do you want me to turn off your night-light?"

"I'll be fine," he said, his tone almost brusque. He slipped down into the bed and reached over and turned off the light.

"See you in the morning," she said.

"Wait, what? You won't be here in the morning too, will you?"

"Yes," she said. "I'll grab a few hours' sleep in the meantime. I'm doing a double shift."

"I've been through enough of those myself. They're not fun."

"Maybe not," she said, "but, trying to help a friend, well, that makes a difference."

"Lucky friend," he called out softly.

"All my friends are lucky," she said, and then she closed his door.

She stood here for a long moment, wondering why the mention of the sketchbooks had brought on that reaction from Finn. She frowned, walked back to her office and jotted a small note about this in his file. It was hard to know with these guys sometimes just what was going on behind that tough-guy facade. They'd been through so much mental stress, so much physical trauma, that you never really understood sometimes who and what these people were on the inside.

So far, Finn had shown himself to be amiable, hard-working, going the extra distance to help himself, to the point that he'd even refused to comment when it was too much. She'd seen the damage afterward. She also knew that Shane was once again working on Finn as well and that structural-integrity stuff was happening. Speaking of, she needed to put a note in the file about his back. She quickly updated his file online and took care of a bunch of paperwork.

She glanced at her watch. The woman she'd relieved for the first part of her shift was coming on soon, and then Fiona herself would head home for a couple hours before showing up for her eight o'clock morning shift. She started to yawn and got up and walked around a little bit to keep her brain active. She did another pass through the hallways, but everything was calm and quiet. It was one of the reasons she didn't particularly like the night shift—she preferred to have something to do all the time.

But then again, she was still here at Hathaway House because it was way less busy than a regular hospital nursing job. She loved the family scenario here so much. She really didn't see herself changing locations anytime soon.

But Finn had brought up an interesting point, even though it's not one he'd meant to. What about a relationship? Was she still hiding? She'd caught her best friend and boyfriend in bed, and that had been enough for her. It had been years ago. It's not that she was horribly religious, but she did expect loyalty and not infidelity while they were together.

Her boyfriend apparently hadn't expected it out of himself at all, just from her.

It had tainted her view of relationships and friendships. She and her girlfriend were obviously no longer friends, and that her boyfriend and her girlfriend had been carrying on behind Fiona's back for months just made it that much more hurtful.

As she sat here in her chair, she wondered about Finn. There was so much to like about him. He'd found a spot in the back of her heart, settled in, made himself at home. Did she like him enough? Or did she not want to go down that pathway? Was it fear of the path? She was very aware of patient-nurse relationships.

One patient had become a little too attached to her, and it had been very painful to separate. He'd taken it terribly when she'd finally been forced to confront him very bluntly with Dani at her side as to what was going on. The shrinks had worked with him for quite a while afterward, but he'd taken it hard.

So now, with her own personal history and the professional history of her relationship with a patient where he had misinterpreted her feelings for him, Finn worried her. Yet she didn't see any similarities between her previous patient and Finn. Maybe she should talk to Dani about it.

With that thought in mind, she sent herself a reminder email to talk to Dani. Fiona should also maybe talk to Dani about the sketchbooks and Finn's odd reaction. Then Fiona heard footsteps in the hallway.

She stepped out to see Becky, her replacement, rushing toward her. The beaming smile of happiness on her face made it all worthwhile. When she held up her finger and flashed the new diamond ring on it, Fiona realized how special Becky's night had been. Becky threw herself into Fiona's arms, and they hugged tight.

"Oh, my goodness. Oh, my goodness," Becky cried out. "We're engaged. We're engaged!"

She was trying to keep her voice down, but, at the same time, she was so ecstatic that it was almost impossible to be quiet. Fiona caught her up into her arms and hugged her again. They moved inside the nurses' station and closed the door, so they wouldn't wake anybody, and Fiona immediately demanded details.

Becky chuckled and said, "We haven't set a date. We don't know anything, except look," and she squealed again. On that note, Fiona couldn't leave right away. She was too hyped, and so was Becky. So Fiona made tea for both of them, but hers was to help her to sleep. They sat and discussed the dinner and the proposal and how special it was. It was obvious that Becky was completely over the moon.

Finally, Fiona gave her friend an extra hug and said, "Now I'm gone. I'll be back in five hours to do my regular shift."

"Go, go, go," Becky said. "And I owe you one big-time."

Fiona waved it off and headed home to her rooms. She was absolutely overjoyed for Becky. She and her beau had been going out for years. They had often talked about marriage but had never come to that sticking point, but now it was almost too good to be true. He worked in town, and Becky worked here, so they had options where they wanted to live, but chances were she would live in town. She would probably not want to do night shifts either if she's newly married.

But that was for Becky and her fiancé to work out. Fiona was thrilled for both of them. She quickly changed into her pajamas, brushed her teeth and crawled into bed. Even though she'd had that last bit of excitement, she fell asleep with a smile on her face. And also with a little pang of loneliness in her heart.

SEVERAL DAYS LATER Finn finally had a few hours to himself and wasn't exhausted enough that he just wanted to lie in bed and cry. It had taken a long time to get here—more than six weeks now—but the last two nights he hadn't woken up in pain, and that had been the best thing ever.

The difference that a good night's sleep made had been astronomical, and, with that, today had been that much easier. He'd had several meetings with his therapist over some of the work that Finn had been doing and whether it was working or not. His medical team members were all really delighted with his progress, whereas Finn couldn't see it except that he was sleeping better now, and he wasn't dealing with as much pain.

Now he had an hour before dinner, and, if he didn't

want to go early to avoid the rush, for the first time in a long time, he wondered what to do with that spare time.

His gaze landed on the sketchbooks to his side. When Fiona had asked him about it earlier, he hadn't known what to say. He hadn't even opened the sketchpad since they'd been purchased and gifted to him.

How terrible was that?

His instant reaction had been guilt and a need to brush it off and to not disclose that he had yet to do anything.

Fear was one of those terrible things that just sat there and ate away at your soul, even for the little things. He remembered being in school and having to do presentations in front of the class, and he couldn't sleep for days as they got closer and closer to the event. He stood up there and stammered, his face turning red, and he'd looked like a fool. It was probably way more embarrassing for everybody else than for him. He was in so much shock that he never did get half of his presentations out. He had the worst stage fright and panic attacks in the world, but he'd grown out of it eventually.

Except when Fiona had questioned him about his art, he'd been back in school again, and the teacher had picked him to answer a question he didn't have an answer for. Such a weird sense of being an adolescent again.

He got up and, using his crutches, brought the sketchbooks and the pencils over to his bed. He tried with his knees up. One knee up. He propped the other one up to use it as a bit of a table. No matter what he did though, it wasn't working. Frustrated, he finally grabbed one of the pillows and put that underneath his sketch pad, and that worked.

He opened to the first page and got out one of his favorite pencils. He'd always preferred a 2B. It wasn't everybody's favorite, but it was his. They were nicely sharpened, but he didn't know quite what to draw. He sat here aimlessly, letting his fingers hold the pencil for a bit, getting used to the feel of it in his hands. And then, closing his eyes, he smiled and let his fingers do their thing. He didn't know how long he sketched—at least ten to fifteen minutes.

He reached for a bottle of water, had a sip and went back to it. Finally, he could see the shape, the turn of the nose, the glint in the eyes. He chuckled. It's not what he had expected to be sketching right now. And certainly it was a rough piece, but at least it was something. He kept working away for another good half hour, and finally, his arms got a little bit on the sore side. He dropped his pencil and shook his hand out.

Needing to move, he got up and hobbled on crutches around the room. He always had to remember to get up and to move, even just a quick turn around the room and several deep breaths in order to keep his muscles fluid. He didn't know how office workers did it. Sitting at a computer all day had to be brutal. Finally, he sat back down again and looked at the sketch. As he studied the face in front of him, he had to admit it wasn't half-bad. It wasn't great. But as a first attempt in ... what? Ten years? It wasn't bad at all.

"So there you are," Dani said, walking in. He held the sketchbook against his chest. She smiled and said, "I'm glad to see you using those."

He studied her face, but, as always, Dani was sheer, wholehearted warmth and a lovely personality. "How could I not?" he asked. "Most of the time I'm so tired. I haven't had any energy to even think about it."

"May I see what you're working on?"

He winced. "You've seen my good pictures," he warned.

"This is nothing like that."

"I've seen some pretty awful sketches that you started out with and tossed, and I've seen some absolutely fantastic pieces you hated that you ripped into shreds," she said with a grin. "And I know you haven't done this for years, so I don't really expect it to be very good. I'm just curious to see what you would choose to draw."

At that, he laughed. "I'm not sure I should be drawing this," he said. "The fact of the matter is, I didn't expect to. But, when I put pencil to paper, that's what came up."

"Tell me more," she said, hitching a hip to rest on his bed. "That sounds like something even better."

He handed it to her. She studied his face for a long moment and then turned to look at the image. Her eyes widened as he watched, and a smile immediately lit up her face. "Wow," she said. "I understand how hard you are on yourself, so I expected you to say it's not very good, but you certainly caught the essence of her."

"That's what I was thinking," he said. "I don't know if it's a picture I want to keep working on or not," he said, "but there's just that light, that little bit that makes Fiona caught right there," he said. "I don't even know how."

"Oh, I do," Dani said lightly, still studying the paper. "You have exceptional talent. I've told you that for years. This is unbelievably good."

"I just forgot everything around me," he said. "There's such a sense of satisfaction when taking something in your mind and putting it on paper."

"Absolutely," she said. "This is fantastic." She handed it back to him. "And you have no idea how happy you've made me to see you sketching again."

"You were behind the sketchbooks anyway," he said. "I

figured that I should do something with them. Otherwise, you'd consider it a waste of money."

"Not really," she said. "I figured that, when you were ready, you'd get there." She tilted her head toward the sketchbook. "And that just proves I was right."

"Ouch," he said with a laugh. "Don't tell her I did this, please."

"No, I won't," she said. "That's personal."

He nodded. "Very."

She smiled and said, "Why don't you start drawing the things that really bug you too? You used to do that way back whenever situations bothered you. You put them down on paper, and sometimes you even ripped them up until you could deal with them."

He looked at her thoughtfully. "I'd forgotten all about that."

"Yeah, remember that scar you had? You kept drawing all these faces, all these self-portraits with the scar, every new one making it bigger and badder and meaner and uglier, as if by putting all that poison from your mind onto the paper, you could dispel some of it. As I recall, it worked too." She hopped off his bed and asked, "Are you coming in for dinner?"

He nodded slowly. "I am. Are you going yourself or are you heading to your house?"

"My dad's finally home. He's been traveling around but is back now."

"The major?" He said, "I have yet to see him."

She spun around and stared at him. "What? Come on then," she said. "Let's go."

Laughing, he hopped up, grabbed his slipper and his crutches, and together they walked to the cafeteria. "Are you sure?" he asked. "He'll probably be surrounded by people."

"My dad is always surrounded by people," she said, sending Finn a sideways look. "He's a very different person than before."

"So I've heard," he said. "It's one of the reasons I really want to see him. I remember what he was like. I also remember how difficult it was to live with him and how sad you always were."

She smiled. "I was. But it's amazing how much he's changed and how much I've changed."

"Well, you have Aaron," Finn said teasingly. "Has your dad got a partner?"

"No, he doesn't, but he does like to tease all the women."

"That's a side I didn't see before either." They got to the double-wide cafeteria doors to hear a cheerful, happy crowd at the food line, but instead, she led him to the deck outside. "You okay to sit out here?"

"Of course," he said. "Why not? It's beautiful out."

She marched him to a large table and said, "Grab a spot where you can get in and out easily, and we'll sit here and wait till the rush arrives. When the crowd goes down, then we can go get some food."

He liked that idea. He propped his crutches beside him and waited until, all of a sudden, a whole group of men came over, and one of them slammed a tray down right beside Finn, making him start.

"Finn?" a loud voice roared.

He looked up in shock. Well, it was the major all right. But not the major who Finn knew. He stood up shakily. "Oh my," he said, staring at the burly man with a huge grin on his face. "Is this really possible? I don't think I ever remember you with a smile before," he joked.

Almost immediately the major's smile fell away. He looked at Dani, back at Finn, nodded and said, "And those days are firmly behind me. Now I smile all the time and I don't even have to try." He reached out and swept Finn into a great big bear hug. Finn hugged him back because he understood those crappy circumstances.

When he finally released him, the major looked at him and shook his head. "Wow. I'm sad to say it, but I'm also very glad that you're here. It's really good to see you, son."

Chapter 9

FIONA WATCHED THE large party at the table just ahead and to the side of her. They all looked to be having so much fun, though a part of her was infinitely jealous, and yet, also very happy for Finn. He seemed to get along with a lot of people very easily. Elliot was even there. Then again, she'd seen the two of them together a lot. And that was good. It was right. Finn needed a buddy. His life was tough enough without that camaraderie those two had. She wondered if she was one of many or if she was special in Finn's mind. From their discussions, it seemed she was special, but …

She'd been taken in before. But Finn wasn't the kind to be deceitful. Her own insecurities led her down that pathway. She didn't have a problem with any of his physical—as he would say—abnormalities. As a nurse, she'd seen so much in her life, and yet, she saw the human courage, that ability to get back up even when you're knocked down, that always amazed her and made her look at people in admiration. Finn more than most. But maybe that's because she had a soft spot for him.

Anna booted her gently under the table. "What are you thinking?"

Fiona pulled herself back to her dinner table and smiled at her friend. "Nothing much," she said smoothly.

But Anna wasn't having any of it. She twisted around so she could see where Fiona had been looking. "Dani looks to be having a fun time tonight. The major is always the life of the party."

Fiona nodded. "I think the major knows Finn."

"Well, that would explain it," Anna said. "How come you're not over there?"

"Why would I be?" Fiona asked.

"Because you and Finn have a thing," Anna said with a great big smile. "Everybody knows it."

"Everybody but me, apparently." She gave a half laugh. "That's not fair. *Something* is between us," she said, "but it's too early to tell just what that is."

"No, that's not quite true," Anna said. "You already know you're in that lovely stage of *Does he, or doesn't he?*" At that, she grinned.

Fiona let out a peal of laughter. She knew she'd been a little too loud when both Dani and Finn turned to look at her. She immediately quieted her voice and gasped, "Oh, my goodness, is it that bad?"

"Absolutely, it is," Anna said. "Just think about it. You mope around all the time when he's not available, and, when you're with him, you light up. He's the first person you want to tell something about your day."

Fiona sat back slightly and nodded. "I hadn't really considered these points. Or that I'm so obvious," she admitted. "I mean, I like him as a person. I like him as a friend. We had a date," she added with a smile, "and I love spending time with him ..."

"And you want him as more than a friend," Anna said with a nod. "And it doesn't matter how much I tell you that it's there, you still won't believe me unless he says something."

"Exactly, and, of course, I'm a little bit distrustful of the patient-nurse relationship," she said, drawing that out to make it more humorous. "And he does have a self-image issue compounding that."

"I think that's one of the biggest things that we find here," Anna said. "Men come in, beaten up by life, and they were all big healthy strapping men beforehand, and who they are now is a completely different person, at least on the outside. Most of the time they have to find that inner strength to fall in love with themselves all over again, as the best person they can be right now."

"And Finn's not there yet," she said.

"The colostomy?"

Fiona nodded. "That's part of it. I think the missing leg is another part but minor. He seems to think the colostomy is very unsexy."

"So, as the girl who potentially could end up sharing his bed, how do you find it?" Only simple curiosity could be heard in Anna's voice.

And, for that reason alone, Fiona answered her. "I couldn't care less," she said. "He's missing a big chunk of muscle from his back and a couple ribs too, but that doesn't make me feel any differently. He's missing his lower right leg. That doesn't make me feel any differently. I'm a nurse," she said with a shrug. "I've seen it all, and I'm not looking for physical perfection. I'm looking for inner strength."

"And we have heard from multiple people with colostomies how they feel about it. You know Sarah here has one, right?"

Fiona nodded. "Yes, I do, and she's adapted well to it by now."

"I think she feels her surgery was a gift, in a way. She's pain-free. She's happy. She's married, and her husband obviously doesn't have a problem with it. You and I both know the world doesn't want to contemplate bodily functions, let alone talk about them, but they're an essential part of healthy living. When bodily functions mess up, it has a drastic effect on us. Honestly, Finn should be grateful. He'd be dead without that colostomy."

"It's so different in our medical world. We talk about this freely. And he is alive today because he had that colostomy. And telling him that is *so* not gonna be helpful," Fiona said with a chuckle. "Although I've said more or less the same thing to him."

Anna nodded. "Again, back to that 'have to work it out themselves' issue."

"Dani bought him some sketchbooks and pencils," Fiona said. "I hope he's started drawing something but no clue. It might take him time."

"And, of course, you're not gonna pry."

"Of course not," she said. "And I'm not even sure that he *is* sketching. It's just that the sketchbooks used to always be off to the side, but he's moved them closer. Maybe I'm wrong. Maybe I'm just hoping he's started drawing again."

"It'd be good for him," Anna said. "Everybody needs an outlet here."

"Right," she said, "it's even more important here."

"I would just keep on the way you're going," Anna said. "He'll get the message."

"Oh, I think he has the message," Fiona said, her lips twitching. "But it takes time, you know."

"Not around here, it doesn't. Not when we all know too well about the fragility of life," Anna said with a smirk. "And not with you. There's no need for time. You're so picky, and yet, you already know you care about Finn. You're a wise woman, probably ready to settle down, yes? You're in your early thirties, and what is he, early to mid-thirties? It's the perfect time for two people, wise to the world, to make better choices now. And, if you want to be together, why would you waste any more moments being apart?" At that, Anna stood, grabbed her tray and said, "I'll see you later."

Fiona nodded. She sat here nursing her cup of coffee as she leaned back and relaxed. It was dinnertime and her evening off. The sun was still high in the sky, creating yet another gorgeous Texas day. It seemed like this was God's country. She looked at the rolling hills, the animals, and caught sight of Stan coming up the stairs. She watched the veterinarian as he came up the far side. He looked more tired than usual. She lifted a hand in greeting, catching his eye.

He smiled and walked over.

"Long day?" she asked.

He nodded. "Long, stressful and sad. I'm gonna grab some food. Do you mind if I join you?"

"Please do," she said. She waited for him to return, feeling better just having somebody here at her table to talk to. She was surrounded by people but had felt very alone for a moment, and there was no need for it because Anna had just left.

It was because of the twenty feet that separated her from Finn. And yet, it wasn't twenty feet—it was miles. Miles of emotional expanse. She didn't know where they were going—*if* they were going anywhere—but she hoped so. She was wondering how long it would take for her to get over her doubts about whether Finn's feelings for her were real or not. She also had to avoid judging him based on her ex's behavior.

She'd been distant with patients, cordial, of course, but never too friendly. Until now. She'd had no choice with him as something between them just clicked. And this time, it was *her* heart that would likely get hurt.

Just then Stan sat down across from her with a plate of roast beef, mashed potatoes, and Yorkshire pudding.

She looked at it and smiled. "I saw all that food, but I just wanted a salad tonight."

"I'm tired and worn out. I have to go back down and check on a very difficult case from this afternoon," he said. "I need the energy." He forked up his first bite of roast beef and sat back as he chewed, a picture of sheer bliss on his face.

She chuckled. "Well, it's nice to know that you're enjoying it."

"I get that, in a lot of medical institutions, the food is one of the biggest complaints. Here, Dani runs a really great cafeteria. And we never ever get shafted on the quality of the food."

"I don't think Dennis would allow it," she said, smiling. "Just think about it. This kitchen's his domain."

"And yet, other chefs are in the back, and he's more the face of the kitchen," Stan muttered around a mouthful of food.

"Exactly," she said.

Just then Dennis appeared at her side. "Hey, did I hear my name called?" He topped off her coffee.

She chuckled. "You did but all good things," she said, "always all good things."

He stopped and watched as Stan had another bite and then asked, "How is it?"

Stan couldn't even answer. He just picked up his free

hand and pinched his thumb and forefinger together in a circle to say, *A-okay.*

Dennis nodded with satisfaction and disappeared again.

"He doesn't need to be collecting dishes, but he's always out here," she said, "always filling up waters and coffees and helping the patients. Just generally being a nice guy."

"And that's what he is," Stan said, "just a generally nice guy. We need more like him in this world."

"True enough," she said. "And it's always hard to know what's going on inside a person versus outside too."

"You're talking about Finn?"

She frowned and then let her irritation slide away. "Yes." She caught the twinkle in Stan's gaze. "Does everybody know?"

"Sure. Why not?" he said. "We do love to see people matched up happily."

"Well, it's too early to be that," she said.

"Nope, not at all," he said. "But you're going through that really interesting kinda-sorta-boyfriend-girlfriend-but-not-quite-there-yet stage," he said. "I find that fascinating. It's like when two animals come together but walk away only to return as if they have absolutely no choice—like magnets. That's you and Finn. I've seen it many times before, and I hope to see it many times again," he said. "And here, with you two, it's definitely obvious. You guys have that electrical surge around you when you come together."

"And it's not just physical?" she murmured in a low tone.

All seriousness fell from Stan's gaze, and he shook his head slowly. "I can see you're feeling very insecure, and, of course, the only way to feel any better about that," he said, "is to talk to him and see if you can work through some of this. And, I imagine, you feel like it's way too early for that."

She gave him a luminous smile and said, "Very wise of you."

"I didn't earn my gray hairs for nothing," he said with a smile.

"So, what's this terrible case downstairs?"

"I've got a female lab that was hit by a vehicle," he said, "and she was pregnant. I had to do a C-section right off the bat because the babies were almost full-term. Then more surgery to try to save her life. Now, of course, we're hand-feeding the pups while we see if the mom can survive and if she'll produce any milk. And also keeping the puppies close to her so that they know who Mom is."

Fiona's heart broke at the thought. "Oh my," she said. "May I come down and see them?"

"Absolutely," he said. "As soon as I finish eating, I have to check on them. I'll be staying close by all night. She's touch-and-go at the moment."

"In which case, you're gonna have puppies to bottle-feed and often," she said.

"Five of them," he said with a smile. "Five wiggly small black newborns that deserve a chance at life."

"Exactly." Then she compulsively said, "If you need somebody to help bottle-feed ..."

"Accepted," he said instantly. At the suddenness of his response, she looked at him and said, "Did you set me up?"

He gave her a bland smile and said, "I always knew that you were a warm, caring, loving person who would do whatever was needed to help. Besides, you won't be alone, and it would be every two hours."

The thought of every two hours made her cringe. It was hard to get a good night's sleep when it was interrupted so often.

He said, "If we have enough people to handle every four hours, you'd only have to get up once in the night."

She smiled at that. "Will you get any sleep?"

"Depends on how many volunteers I get," he said craftily. "And the mom is also a major part of my concern because life will be so much easier on those pups if Mom survives too."

"I can't imagine," she said. She settled back, sipped her second cup of coffee and waited until he was done.

As soon as he was, he hopped to his feet and said, "Ready?"

She nodded and quickly grabbed his and her trays, carried them to Dennis, who met her halfway across the room to take them from her. Then Stan came over and said, "Come on. Let's go." He didn't slow his pace. She gave a wave to Finn as she walked past, but she raced to keep up with Stan.

Dani noticed and called out, "Stan, any update?"

"Five pups. Mom's in tough condition." And then he was gone.

Fiona could hear Dani giving an explanation to her dinner companions, obviously having heard the news earlier.

Then Fiona got really busy as she walked into the back of the vet clinic and was immediately handed a tiny black wiggly-worm pup that wasn't any bigger than her hand and a minuscule dropper and was asked to start feeding. And with now two of these guys tucked up against her, she fed them both with eyedroppers, then she closed her eyes and cuddled them close.

"Do you think Stan would mind if I go down?" Finn asked Dani in a low voice.

She smiled, leaned over and whispered, "He's probably dying to get volunteers if it's puppy-feeding time. Over the years, I've helped many, many times," she admitted. "Sometimes we have kittens, sometimes puppies, sometimes ducklings. He takes in anything that needs help, and, in this case, the mother is badly in need of help." She motioned downstairs. "Go if you want to."

He nodded and shifted his chair back.

She leaned closer and whispered, "By the way, are you going for Fiona or for the puppies?"

His lips twitched. "Maybe both?"

Her laughter rang out across the table. "I'm delighted to hear that," she said. "Go have fun." She turned back to her father.

Finn realized the discussion at the table didn't include him now and struggled to his feet with his crutches and then made his way downstairs, wondering if he could seriously do anything to help Stan or Fiona or the mother dog or if he would be in the way. The stairs were a challenge, so he took the elevator and dropped down to the veterinarian clinic. When he made his way in through the double doors, he stopped, stunned to see Fiona curled up in a corner with two of the tiniest black puppies possible in her arms, sleeping. Eyedroppers were beside her.

He turned to one of the vet assistants and said, "I heard helping hands were needed."

The woman—her uniform name tag read Babette—looked up at him and smiled. "I think all five puppies are okay for the moment, but, if you want to come and love one," she said, "we're more than happy to have that happen.

Then we're gonna tuck them back up against Mom."

He glanced over to see Fiona's eyes open, staring at him, the depth of her gaze full of love and emotion from seeing and holding these puppies.

He accepted the tiny bundle as soon as he was seated beside her. He cuddled it close and whispered to it constantly. "It's okay, little one. It's been a rough beginning, but you'll make it." The little guy didn't even murmur. He just curled up as much as he could, seeking warmth, and slept. Finn glanced at the puppies nestled high on Fiona's bosom and smiled. "Your two look very happy."

"They're adorable," she said in the softest of voices. "New life like this, it's so precious."

"I can't argue with that," he said. "They've had a rough time of it, but, with any luck, they'll be fine."

"I'm hoping so," she said, reaching up to gently stroke one, then the other. "They don't take in very much food at a time, so they have to be fed on a regular basis."

"Are you gonna get up and come down later and feed them?"

"I think I will," she said. "It depends on how many volunteers they need. I'll come back before bed anyway and do one more round and then see."

"Do all five have to be done at once, or can they be done in rounds?"

Babette answered, "Two of us can handle five babies," she said. "They don't take very long to feed. So, if need be, I can do it myself."

"And Stan said he was gonna stick around close because of Mom?" Fiona said.

Babette nodded. "Mom's really struggling. She may have to go back into surgery, but we're gonna do our best to not have to."

Just then Stan came back out, looked at the puppies and smiled. "That's what they need, warmth, love, food, and as much time as they can have."

"How is she?"

"She's holding," he said. "I'm cautiously hopeful. Depends if she can make it through tonight."

"Right," Fiona said. She looked over at the little guy in Finn's arms. "This guy seems quite content too."

Finn stared down at the little one. He was curled up in the crook of Finn's arm, high on his chest. It wasn't the most comfortable position for him, but he couldn't have cared less while gently stroking the velvety-soft ears, looking at the tiny little face. "Hard to believe these guys are gonna be labs."

"They're just all wrinkled-up pieces of love at the moment," Stan said. "If you guys want to give them back to Babette, I'll put them in with Mom."

"Is it safe to leave her with them?"

"In this case, yes, and Babette will sit in there and will do her work beside Mom and babies. Babette can keep an eye on Mom. These little guys won't really move much right now, and the closer they are to Mom, the better."

Babette came out so they could hand off the puppies to her. Finn looked at the huge female black lab, tubes coming and going from her, obvious stitches showing on her shaven belly, and even a cast on a back leg. She looked to be in seriously rough shape, but it was almost like something about her softened when the puppies were tucked up against her. He imagined that, if she was aware in any way, she'd consider this part of the reward for trying to survive. He looked at Babette. "Do we know anything about what happened?"

"No," she said. "Somebody saw her get hit by a vehicle. They picked her up, put her in the truck bed and brought her in. The fact that we got her as soon as we did is the good news, but we haven't located an owner yet."

"If there is one," Fiona said.

"Too often there isn't, or, if there is, they don't want to admit it, in case they get stuck with the vet bill."

"And do you run a lot of charity work through here?" Finn asked.

"We do, indeed, and Dani funnels a lot of financial assistance to us as well," Babette said. "It's the only way to help those who don't have anybody to help them."

As soon as he handed his pup off, Finn felt bereft.

Fiona gave a heavy sigh. "I didn't want to hand them over," she confessed as soon as Babette disappeared with her two.

"I know," he said, "I was just thinking that. Like there's a hole in my heart already."

She looked up and smiled. "Sad, isn't it?"

"I think it's good," he said in all seriousness. "Think about it. Somebody needs to love these little guys."

"They all deserve love. We all do," she said firmly. She moved toward the door. "Are you coming, or are you staying here?"

"I'm coming," he said. With his crutches once again under his arms, he followed her down the hallway. She stopped, looked outside and said, "I don't know where you're going, but I'm gonna go outside and visit with Lovely and Appie. They're right there at the fence again."

"Perfect idea," he said. His mind buzzed with the picture that he'd seen of Fiona holding the babies. Part of him itched to return to his room and sketch her in that pose, but drawing a picture of her versus spending time with her? Well, there was really no contest. Outside with the animals, he laughed at Lovely's antics as she danced with joy at seeing them. As soon as they were close, she came over and shoved her face through the rails. Appie, not to be outdone, came too.

"We don't have any treats," he said.

"No, but we have long grass." She bent and snapped off several big clumps and handed it to the critters. Both of them immediately accepted their treat with joy. She smiled, her arms crossed on top of the railing and said, "It's so beautiful to see them here."

"Having the animal interaction," he said, "makes this a very special place."

"Doesn't it? Now you know why I am so happy to work here."

"And here I thought it was because of the patients," he teased.

She laughed. "Most patients, yes. Some patients are special, and some are special in other ways," she said, her tone turning wry. "But, on the whole, we've been very blessed. Dani has had good luck in bringing in people who are at the right stage of life to take advantage of what we have to offer."

"I guess that's the trick, isn't it? If you're not ready, it doesn't matter what you are offered here because you don't accept it." He was thinking about how long it had taken him to ask Dani for a bed, how it had taken Elliot to come to that path ahead of Finn to show him the way and why that was surprising because he always used to be a bit of a trendsetter. In this case, it seemed like he was behind the curve.

And then he realized it wasn't that he was behind the

curve—he was literally just behind. Insecure, worried about his future, having trouble dealing with progress. He worried about his progress—or lack of it. He couldn't do a whole lot back then about moving forward faster, but he was grateful that Elliot had convinced him to come because Finn couldn't imagine being anywhere else now.

"Now that you've been here for as long as you have," she said, "how are you?"

"Much, much better," he said. "The night cramps have eased, and that's made it much easier to sleep, which makes the days much nicer too."

"Of course," she said, "and physiotherapy will continue to help you to improve."

"I think the thing about physio here is everything seems so much worse before it ever gets better. So I'm definitely not at the better stage yet," he admitted. "But I'm in a nice place to be as I no longer feel worse every day."

On that note, there was an awkward silence as they both stood here, elbow to elbow, but not quite touching as they stared out at the landscape around them.

"Dani's built something very special," he said, almost as if filling the gap of silence.

"She has."

"Do you think you'll stay here forever?"

"Not forever," she said with a smile. "I'd like to have a family one day. But I'm certainly here until my life changes."

"Sometimes you have to move in order to make a change," he murmured.

"That's very true," she said. "And, if that's the case, I'm in no hurry. There's lots for me to learn and to do, and to feel rewarded by my work here, and by the people I meet. I don't have to be always doing something or feeling like I'm appreciated, but it's lovely to be a part of a big machine like this that can still do so much good for everyone."

"Very true."

"What about you?" she asked. "What are your plans?"

"I'm not exactly sure I have any," he said. "I'm still here for at least another two months—I presume anyway. I haven't had an update from my medical team, but I don't really have any plans afterward. I was hoping that maybe, when I came here, I would find enlightenment in some way or form that would lead me down the right path for me now, after the navy," he said with a mocking tone. "And so far it hasn't happened."

"Give it time," she said with a smile. "You never know what might happen while you're here."

"Yeah?" he said, looking at her. "Like what?"

She just gave him a mysterious smile that hit him right in the heart and said, "Maybe wait and see."

Chapter 10

FIONA HAD NO real reason for leading him on except that she truly believed in the power of healing. When people healed their physical bodies, they also helped to heal their emotional and mental bodies—and vice versa—and that led to making decisions and seeing clarity in their lives. She had no doubt Finn would sort himself out, just like every other person she'd met here. And she'd met hundreds by now. It was amazing as she looked back along the years of all the patients who had come through Hathaway House's doors and just how well so many had done here.

Days later, when she walked into his room to see him quickly closing his sketchbook and putting it beside him, she realized he truly was back at his artwork. She smiled brightly at him and said, "Do those pencils work well for you?"

"They do," he said noncommittally.

She had to do a full checkup on him. By the time she had written down her notes, she said, "I didn't get to see you yesterday," she murmured.

"No," he said, "my therapy has switched again, and I have to admit to it being pretty rough." But there was no strain in his voice, and he was still as friendly as ever.

She motioned at his belly. "Any problems with the co-lostomy?"

"Only that it exists," he said, but a new teasing tone was

in his voice, as if he might be finally coming to terms with it.

"At least you only have one," she said. "It could be worse. You could have two."

"And I've only just recently come to understand that," he said. "Who knew you could have two bags, not just one?"

She chuckled. "I'll still get you a pink polka-dot one."

"*Yuck.*" He shook his head. "Unless there's something macho male out there that'll help, don't bother," he said with a smile.

"As more and more people end up with this problem," she said, "someone will get creative and will make all kinds of designs."

"Right, and I guess I'll never get rid of this, will I?"

"They do these temporarily for some patients, while other areas of the body heal or have to be reconstructed. I'm not sure what the situation is in your case, but I suspect this is permanent."

"My surgeon said it was permanent, but I keep hoping …"

"You can hope," she said, "but stay within the realm of reality."

"Right," he said, "and that means this is permanent."

She studied his face for a long moment, but he didn't appear to be anywhere near as down and depressed about it. "Sounds like you may be getting used to the fact that it exists."

"Well, I'm not screaming and depressed and crying about it, if that's what you mean," he said briskly. "And, as I improve in other areas, it is easier to look at something like that and realize that I've done everything I can and that I can't improve it anymore, so I'll have to live with it."

"Good," she said. "Speaking of which, I understand the

prosthetic fitting is happening in the next week."

"I hope so," he said. "I'll finally see how this latest surgery did."

"Well, here's to hoping," she said. "I know sometimes it takes a couple attempts, but it would make such a huge difference in your mobility."

"It always did," he said. "Even though my stump swelled up, I didn't want to let go of it."

She motioned to the sketchbook. "How's the drawing going?" At that, she could feel him withdrawing again.

He shrugged and said, "As ugly as I expected it to be."

She smiled, picked up her tablet and said, "You'll just get better," she said, "like with everything else."

And she walked out. There was something very secretive about him and his sketchbook, as if he didn't want her to see it. Having seen the drawing he'd done in Dani's office, Fiona couldn't imagine it being very ugly. But, if he was using his drawing as a therapy that could rid him of some of his depression, then maybe he wasn't drawing pretty pictures either. He needed time alone to do his thing.

As she walked down the hallway, Dani walked toward her. "How are you doing?"

"I'm fine," she said, "but you look serious."

"The one patient we had who gave you some issues," she said, "do you remember him—Ziegler? He sent a letter and a lawyer's note."

Fiona froze. "A lawyer's note?"

"He's attempting to sue us for our handling of the situation."

Her stomach sank. "He's the one who got a little too infatuated with me. I didn't know how to get out of it," she said. She reached up a hand, rubbed her forehead and said,

"What was I supposed to do?"

"Our lawyers will handle it," Dani said gently. "I just wanted to let you know that this was in progress."

"And that's likely to stop me from ever being friendly with anyone again," she cried out. "What a horrible turn of events."

"No," Dani said firmly. "Some people—like Finn—need it."

"The trouble with Finn," she said, her voice harsher than she wanted it to be, "is I don't want him to see me in that light. I really care about him." Lowering her voice, she said, "Finn is not like Ziegler at all. I didn't see him as anything other than a patient. But Finn's different."

"And Finn would handle the situation differently. Ziegler was dealing with more than rejection, and my lawyers will make that very clear. He received the best treatment he could possibly get here, and he wanted a whole lot more than he got. That's the end of it."

She said it so firmly that Fiona wanted to believe her. To a certain extent she did, but it was depressing, nonetheless. "Well, I hope he doesn't cause any more trouble, and that can be the end of it," she said slowly. "Has it ever happened before?"

Dani shook her head. "No, it's the first case."

"But it does set a precedent for all of us now to look at our relationships with the patients and worry that we'll be taken in the wrong way."

"One in hundreds," Dani said. "Really, that's about to be expected. We can't expect to walk away from something like that scot-free. We would love it if it would never happen, but you know what the world's like."

"I know," Fiona said, "but I can't tell you how much I

regret that happening in the first place."

"And we all know that," Dani said. "Anyway, carry on with your rounds. I've got to go back to the office."

Fiona stood in the hallway and watched as Dani headed to the reception area. Suddenly feeling more depressed and bereft, she walked to the front to see if Racer was there. Surprise, surprise, he was. His little tail wagged like crazy when he saw her.

She picked up his basket, petting him with her free hand, and asked, "How do you feel about coming to visit with me?" She had a lot of notes to enter, and having him around would be a help. She carried him back and placed him on the desk beside her. He just lay here, his huge eyes blinking at her as she gently stroked his ears. She spent a few minutes cuddling him before working on her notes.

When she looked up, Dani sneaked in, taking one look at Racer and snagging him for herself. "Another patient needs him." And she disappeared.

Fiona chuckled. "It was definitely a huge plus with him being here."

On that note, a grumbling *meow* came from the doorway, and she looked around to see the latest addition to the therapy animals—the three-legged cat, a big Maine coon that had his ways fixed, sat and stared at her. It reminded her of the puppies. Fiona had been at the clinic several days in a row, helping out, but hadn't been needed thereafter. She'd sent a message to Stan asking for an update. She didn't expect to hear anytime soon, but she should probably make it there on her lunch hour and see if she could visit with them.

Finally, she was done with the paperwork, and it was time to do another round again. She started at the other end so she would end up at Finn's. By the time she was done, a couple patients taking longer than normal, she was tired and ready to be done with her day. When she finally entered Finn's room, he had his sketchbook open across his lap, and he'd nodded off. She hesitated at the doorway. If he didn't want her to see his sketchbooks, then she didn't want to look, but she needed to wake him up.

Keeping her eyes averted, she walked up to him, gently picked up his arm and took his blood pressure. He woke up with a jerk and stared at her, blinking owlishly. She smiled at him. "Just rounds."

He nodded, closed the sketchbook and shifted. "I didn't realize I was so tired."

"Apparently," she said. "Are you sure you're not doing too much?"

"I probably am," he admitted. "But, once you start seeing those first signs of progress, you just want to get to the end as fast as you can."

"This is definitely a case where the turtle wins the race," she warned.

"And you know you can tell me that until you're blue in the face, and it still won't make a difference as to how I feel."

She smiled gently at him. "You and everybody else in this place."

He chuckled and said, "I'm also very hungry. Is it almost dinnertime?"

"Almost," she said. "I'm off now."

"Will you have dinner with me?" he asked in a rush.

She looked at him, smiled and said, "Sure. I'll go home, get changed and what? Meet you in the dining room?"

He nodded. "If we're early, we can always have coffee first."

She checked her watch and said, "How about we meet in forty-five minutes?"

"Good, and, if I start now, I might make it on time," he joked.

She grinned and turned and walked away, but her footsteps were lighter. She wasn't exactly sure what she'd caught sight of in his sketch, and she didn't really want to analyze it because he'd closed it as soon as he'd been aware of it, but it had been the start of a woman's face. She just didn't know what woman. Fiona suspected Dani, but who knew? Fiona hoped he didn't have any intentions for Dani because Dani's heart was definitely locked with Aaron's. Those two were a perfect match.

But Finn and Dani went way back, so who knew just how deep the heart went? And maybe they were just good friends. Still, it bothered Fiona. It bothered her a lot. She couldn't stop thinking of anything else when she showered and got dressed in another summer dress. As she headed out from her place to meet him in the dining room, she tried to let it go, but, as she walked up, Finn already was seated with Dani at his side. Dani looked at Fiona, smiled, then leaned over, kissed Finn on the cheek, and got up and left. At that way-too-friendly gesture, Fiona's heart sank.

"YOU LOOK ABSOLUTELY stunning," Finn said in admiration. "That dress with the blues and greens flowing around you is gorgeous."

"Thank you," she said with a smile. "I didn't realize you and Dani were that close."

"Not that close," he said. "But we've been friends for

decades. Or at least it seems like that. I don't want to count too close to see if it really is that long or not."

"Maybe two decades," she said.

"Okay, but it feels longer," he said with a smile. "And I know how happy she is with Aaron."

"She is, indeed," Fiona said, taking a seat beside him. "Have you checked out what's on the menu tonight?"

"Greek," he said. "These theme nights are absolutely to die for."

"Dani has always done a great job with the food budget here," she said. "And Dennis keeps us all coming back for more."

"A happy tummy is a happy system," he said. "Do you want to sit for a bit, or do you want to eat first?"

"You were the one who was starving earlier."

"I am, that's why I'm having the coffee, to try and take that sting back a bit."

"Then we'll sit and wait until you finish your coffee," she said. "I'm in no rush." She looked over at the sideboard and said, "Actually, there's fresh juice. Do you want one?"

"SURE," HE SAID. He watched as she walked over to get water first. The dress flowed freely around her, wrapping her curves and showing off her long legs. He wondered at her questions about his relationship with Dani and realized Fiona had probably seen the kiss Dani had given him. But there'd been a reason for that. Dani was cheering him on in every aspect of his life. She always had. Matter of fact, she was one of the best cheerleaders he'd ever met. But he didn't want Fiona to get the wrong idea.

At the same time, Dani had also explained about the problem with the one patient, and he realized just how much of an issue him liking Fiona might be for her. To think that a pending lawsuit would add to her sense of guilt, that bothered him. It was just more crap for her and Dani to deal with that wasn't necessary. When she returned with two glasses of water and then disappeared again, he watched, loving every step she took and the way the dress molded to her body.

"Dresses like that should be banned," he decided. "But I'm glad they haven't been." They were way too sultry, and she had the body for it. And with her hair braided down the center of her back like that, she was very beautiful.

When she returned with two large glasses of juice and sat down again, she looked at him, a puzzled look on her face, and asked, "What's the matter?"

He lifted both eyebrows. "The only thing that matters," he said, "is you're too beautiful to believe."

She stared at him, pleased. "Thank you, I think," she said. "But what you see is what you get."

"I wish," he muttered. He caught her sudden surprised look. He shrugged and said, "You know I care for you."

"Well, I know something is there between us," she said lightly. "It's just a matter of what that is."

"Dani told me about that lawsuit." He could see her expression dim.

"It's one of the low points in my life," she said quietly. "I would never deliberately lead anybody on, and I would never wish such emotional pain on anyone."

"And yet, I think we're all forgetting the fact that, because of that, he healed and worked harder and faster than he ever could have before. Of course, he's only thinking that the carrot he expected was pulled away by you, instead of giving the carrot to him, but the real plus here is the fact that he did so very well."

"Maybe," she said, "but I'm no carrot for anyone, and the fact that he thought I was a prize at the end of his day makes me feel quite icky."

"I didn't mean it that way," he said gently. "But knowing that you were there is what helped him to heal so much faster."

"Maybe." But her gaze turned almost inward, and he kicked himself for having mentioned it. "Just in case," he said suddenly, "I don't want you to compare the fact that I really like being around you and really enjoy spending time with you as similar to his problem."

And once again, he could feel her shuttering back and closing off. "Seriously," he said in an attempt to regain lost ground.

She nodded and said, "It's a painful topic. Let's change it. Are you ready for dinner?"

He accepted the change of conversation and nodded. And, in his wheelchair, he twisted and headed over toward the entrance line to the food. Dennis was there. As he smiled up at the other man, he asked, "Are you ever not here?"

"Sometimes," he said. "I always try to be here for dinnertime. My mama didn't raise any fools." At that, he cracked up laughing. The dinner looked so good, and, by the time Dennis had set up Finn with a nice portion of souvlaki and Greek potatoes, he was looking forward to getting back to his table and diving in. He could have seconds or thirds if he wanted to, and tonight he might.

Traveling carefully with the tray on his lap, he headed back to his table. As he turned to look around the corner to see where Fiona was, she still talked to Dennis, his face lit up even more as he spoke to Fiona, making Finn's own heart clamp down. She knew so many people here, was friendly with so many people that he sometimes felt a little out of the loop. But, then again, that's probably how she felt about the relationship between him and Dani. And how was he to explain what that longtime friendship was actually like?

He knew he wanted to continue this discussion, but he also knew it wouldn't be that easy. When he looked up the second time, she wound her way toward him, carrying her own tray. He quickly emptied his tray, much preferring to eat off the table, like a real dining room. She did the same and then moved both trays to the side. As she sat back down, she sniffed her plate and smiled. "I do love Dennis's cooking."

"Maybe you should marry him," he said, half joking.

She shot him an odd look. "That wouldn't work out so well," she said quietly. "Dennis has been here for a long time. He's a good friend."

Feeling small for his comment—when he'd intended it as a joke, but it had fallen flat—he just nodded. He had to wonder if one of the reasons they fed the patients so well here was, by feeding one appetite, it helped to keep another at bay. He was no saint, and he'd loved many women in his lifetime, but he also knew that the time for short-term relationships were long over for him. That's not who he was anymore, and it hadn't been who he was for a long time. Across from him, Fiona sat, elegant, and yet, sweet, classy and funny. There was just so much to like about her, and he felt like a grumbling teenager.

"You've stopped eating," she said lightly.

With a start, he pulled himself back to his plate, grinned

and said, "Well, that will never do. Dennis might be insulted." He dove back in.

"Have you been in the pool yet?"

He shook his head and forked up another bite. "I've been in the hot tub a couple times a week for the muscle knots, until they eased up, but I haven't had a chance to do hydrotherapy yet. I really want to."

"It's probably coming soon then," she said. "Just talk to your therapist about it."

"I keep forgetting," he said. "It just seems now that I'm a little busier how I lose track of things I want to do."

She seemed to let that slide for a moment; then she looked at him, her head cocked slightly to the side, and in a quizzical voice asked, "So much to do?"

He nodded. "I haven't really told you much," he said, "but the more of my artwork I get back into doing, the more I feel like doing, and it becomes all-consuming. I had that problem before. I could sit in front of a movie, and I'd sketch away, but, by the end of the movie, I wouldn't remember anything of what had gone on because I'd become so involved in my artwork."

"That sounds wonderful," she said. "Isn't that a good thing?"

"I'm not sure it is," he said slowly. "Sometimes it seemed like hours would go by. I hadn't thought I'd ever get back to it again, and I'm not sure I want to get back into it that intently," he said. "But it is an incredible feeling when you come back out of that fugue to realize what you've created."

"I don't have a creative bone in my body," she announced. "And so I'm incredibly envious of what you can do."

"You don't know anything I can do yet," he said, laughing.

"Not quite," she said. "Dani has a picture that you did of the horses on the back of her office door."

That stopped him for a moment. He stared at her and asked, "Really?"

She nodded. "Absolutely."

He frowned. "I don't remember doing it for her."

"Well, it's there," she said. "Whenever you get back to her office, you can take a look."

"I'll do that," he said. "So, did you like it?"

"No," she said, teasing. "I loved it. The freedom the horses personify—it's as if they came alive off the page. You could just see them moving across the wall. It was really spectacular."

He settled back with a smile at the corner of his lips. "I was wondering about going pro," he said, "but always that voice inside my head said I wasn't that good."

"You are beyond good enough," she said. "I don't know how one does something like going pro, especially in this digital age," she said, "but, if there was any way you could, wow."

"I've tried some digital art," he said, "it doesn't give me the same satisfaction as with a pencil."

"Makes sense to me," she said. "I mean, I used to love Lego blocks. Yet the computer games based on them don't appeal the same to me. Still, the younger generation, I guess they seem to take to it just fine."

He nodded. "I've always been so busy that I didn't have much time for video games."

"And it's never been something I ever wanted to do. I sit at the computer enough during the day. In the evening," she admitted, "I'd rather go for a swim."

"Speaking of which," he said, "I think when I return to my room, I'll send a couple emails to see if I can get the pool added to my options. In the evenings, it would be really lovely to go for a swim."

"And there's no reason you shouldn't," she said. "There are rules, like regarding safety, but, other than that, you should be free to use the pool as you want."

He nodded and then thought about something and slowly lowered his fork. "What about the colostomy?"

She nodded. "You're not stopped from all water sports just because you have that."

"But it might be visible," he said, almost blanching at the thought.

She gazed at him steadily. "And? Your stump will be too."

He frowned at that, thought about it, and nodded. "I guess that's what it's all about, isn't it? My body is no longer what it used to be."

"No," she said, "it's better. It's a survivor. What happened to it had knocked it down, but it didn't stay down. You got back up again, and you're still taking steps forward. That's what counts."

He smiled at her and said, "I knew there was a reason I liked you."

Chapter 11

FIONA REMEMBERED FINN'S words long after she'd gone to bed. She lay here under her blankets, wondering. It was a thought that she kept with her through the night and even when she got up the next morning to start work again. She wondered if he would go to Dani's office and take a look at the picture to see if he remembered it now that Fiona had described it. As it was, she didn't have the chance of doing much thinking throughout the day because she was so busy. And maybe that was a good thing.

By the time her shift was done, she sank back in her office chair, stared up at Helen, who was coming in for the late afternoon shift and said, "Wow, I haven't even had a chance to take a breather."

Helen nodded. "Hopefully you took care of it all," she said, smiling broadly, "so my shift's easier."

"Maybe," she said. "We had two people move out today. We had one new arrival, and one is coming in tomorrow. The new arrival is somebody to keep an eye on." They quickly went over his file, and, as soon as that was done, Fiona stood, stretched and said, "You know what? I think I'll go for a swim."

"They were introducing a bunch of patients to the pool today," Helen said. "I saw them as I walked across."

"Was Finn there?"

Helen looked thoughtful. "I'm not sure if he was or not."

"He was going to ask for permission to go in the pool," she said. "Hopefully he got it."

It was on her mind as she headed downstairs and past the pool. She kept a close eye on it to see if a session was going on. She was allowed to swim after-hours, but, if some of the patients were there working, she didn't want to interrupt them. She didn't see Finn when she walked over to her place, so she decided that the cool splash and the gentle movement of the water was exactly what she needed. She was tired and just stressed enough after her rough day so that a swim would be a perfect answer.

Back at her place, she changed into her bathing suit, grabbed her pullover dress and her towel, and put sandals on her feet. As she headed back to the pool, she could feel her body already craving the cool sensation of the water and the peacefulness of floating. She dropped her towel on one of the benches, kicked off her shoes, pulled her dress over her head and headed toward the shallow end. Her hair was still in a braid, which was perfect for swimming. She stepped down slowly, looking around; a couple people were at the far end. As she hit the bottom step, she noted somebody at the side too. She glanced over to see Finn. She stopped in delight. "I see you got permission to come in the pool."

He nodded slowly, his gaze studying her face. She quickly ducked under the water, suddenly feeling shy. When she swam closer, he said, "Yes, I got permission today, and I'm glad I came. I was tired, almost too tired to make the effort, but I wouldn't have missed that vision for the world."

FINN WATCHED THE wash of color rise up her face before she quickly sank into the water. Not only was she beautiful inside but she was stunning outside. A gorgeous face with a long slim body and she swam like a fish. Even though he was a hell of a swimmer himself, he took time to admire her form as she moved through the water, her arms cutting cleanly as they rose to the surface and back in again.

He was already tired from his PT workout in the pool and was enjoying floating and moving around. It was amazing how easy it was to navigate in the water. It buoyed him and made him feel so much more capable, even with his colostomy bag. The stoma had a space ring to connect the bags he used to his body, but even then it was perfectly safe to be in a shower or the pool. He was a little self-conscious about it, but other people hadn't even made a comment. This was a beautiful place to be, and, if this is what rehab was, he didn't want to leave. Finally, he stroked through the water and then paddled toward her.

"It's good to see you here," she said quietly as she tread-ed water. "Also good that you're out in the open and not trying to hide."

He knew what she meant. "It was awkward at first," he admitted. "Everything above the waist is in better shape," he said, "but at the waistline and below the knee?" He shook his head.

"Neither matter," she said gently.

"And I'm slowly realizing that," he said. "For that, I ap-preciate this place and what Dani's built here. The joy and the healing she's brought to everyone. It's been a pretty incredible time here already."

"And that's why so many people have great experiences here. You've learned to become much more open, much more accepting. As soon as you become more accepting, others do too."

"And I would have said, as soon as they became more accepting, then I did too," he said humorously.

"But you know that's not true," she said. "It's the other way around." She hopped up to sit on the edge of the pool beside him, water dripping down her silky skin.

He deliberately looked away.

"As soon as you learn to love yourself, you learn to become more open," she said. She looked up and waved at Dennis.

"What is he doing?" Finn asked in amusement.

"Looks like he's taking orders," she said.

"Surely not."

"Dennis is one of those people who absolutely loves being here," she said. "He goes over, above and beyond the call of duty at all times. And it's incredibly lovely to see."

"You're not kidding," he said. "Like, wow. What do you think he's taking orders for?"

"I rather imagine something cool and wet, and, if we're lucky, treats to go with it."

He looked at her. "You wouldn't tease me about that, would you?"

She started to laugh.

Dennis looked at her and said, "Nice to see you in a good mood."

"I'm sorry. I've been a little down lately," she said, her laughter slowing, "but I'm doing better."

"You should know that the lawsuit was dropped."

She stared at him in surprise. "Seriously?"

It wasn't much of a surprise to Finn that everybody knew about it because the medical personnel and others here were apparently a tight-knit family, and he kept seeing the proof of it every day. He looked at her and said, "Would that make you feel better?"

"It would make me feel a lot better," she said. "I desperately tried not to do anything wrong here," she said in a low tone. "And, when something like that happens, it completely wipes you out. You don't know how you could have done things differently. I didn't want to hurt him. I really didn't."

"No, and I think the bottom line is, he did so much better because you were here," Dennis stated. "He'll get over it."

She nodded. "Maybe, but I'd just as soon not get into that scenario in the first place."

"Just so you know," Finn said, "I'm stating again that I'm not part of that same scenario."

Startled, she turned to look at him, and he caught the nervousness in her gaze, knowing that maybe she had been thinking that.

He grabbed her hand and said, "I'm not. I'm perfectly capable of understanding who and what is responsible for where I'm at, how I've improved and how I haven't improved, and where I need to improve. And it has nothing to do with an improper emotional connection to you. I know exactly how I feel about you, and it's not related to my health."

He watched as the smile bloomed across her face, making his heart beat rapidly. She leaned across, kissed him gently on his cheek and said, "I hope so."

Just then Dennis interrupted. "None of that. Those of us without partners suffer terribly when we watch all this lovey-dovey stuff happening around us."

She chuckled, smiled and changed the subject. "So, what are you taking orders for?"

"What do you want?" he asked.

"I want coffee, if possible," Finn asked. "And, if there happens to be any treats, I won't turn those down either."

Dennis chuckled. "Do you need a light treat, like a muffin or cinnamon bun, or do you need like a triple-decker sandwich kind of treat?"

"Oh, man," Finn said. He looked at the clock and then shook his head. "It's already almost five, maybe we shouldn't have anything."

"Nonsense," Dennis said. "I'll bring you a sweet treat and a cup of coffee. And then, when you guys eat around sixish, if you want more dessert, you can have that afterward." And, with that, he took off.

She turned to face Finn and said, "As you can tell, he's a happy camper here."

"I really love that," he said. "There's absolutely no sense of being in a position that's beneath him or feeling like he's a servant. I really, really appreciate that attitude."

"That's definitely not how Dennis views his world here." She smiled and stretched back, leaving her legs in the water, but her body was stretched out on the concrete behind her.

"Don't you want something to protect your skin?" he asked.

"No," she said, "I just want to stretch out and feel the wind and the breeze and the sunshine on my body. It's been a really long, hard day."

"I'm sorry if I added to that."

She laughed out loud. "It's been a long hard day because of inventory and catching up on patient records. It's been a long hard day because of filing and documentation management and computers that wouldn't work and keyboards that got coffee spilled on them so they got cranky and a mouse, a cordless mouse that ran out of batteries that I couldn't find. It was just one of those days."

He patted her hand and said, "Then close your eyes and rest."

And that's what she did.

He sat here, beyond content, keeping an eye on her, watching the rest of the world go by. When Dennis returned ten minutes later, he brought over a small table and set it up beside them and plunked down a tray with two large coffees and a plate with the largest darn cinnamon bun Finn had ever seen, cut into four pieces.

Finn smiled and said, "Dennis, I do want to say what a pleasure it is to see your smiling face every day."

"And yours," Dennis said. "Sometimes people arrive here thinking their world has completely collapsed. But, by the time they leave," he said, "it's amazing just how much they have grown and changed."

"And I'm halfway there," Finn said. "I'm not all the way, but I'm getting there." He motioned at Fiona. "Of course, she's a wonderful help in the healing department."

Dennis chuckled. "Any time your heart is touched, it's a help. But, in a place like this, it's always very special." Just then he laughed and pointed and said, "Look at who's here." He gave a slight whistle.

Finn turned to see a large three-legged dog with a prosthetic on her fourth leg, walking toward him. The great big massive black Newfoundlander, her tail wagging, came over to greet Dennis.

"Now does she love you," Finn asked, "because it's you, or does she love you because she knows you're connected to food?"

Dennis bent down, gave her a huge hug, scratched be-

141

hind her ears and buried his face in her neck. When he lifted his face, he said, "I hope the first, but I know for sure the second is at least part of it. This is Helga," he said.

Finn reached out to greet Helga and laughed when he saw the drool coming off the side of her face. "Wow, look at that," he said.

"She's a bit of a spitter," Dennis said, "but we love her anyway."

"Look at her stump too," Finn said. "She handles that prosthetic really well."

"She does, and, when she doesn't have it, she doesn't seem to care either," Dennis said. He gave her a couple good scratches and stood and said, "And I'm back to work." He disappeared.

Fiona sat up to give Helga a big cuddle, and then Helga laid down right beside her—and half on her. She gave a shriek of laughter.

"Is the dog allowed in the pool?" Finn asked.

"I am not exactly sure about that," she said, tilting her head to the side. "It would probably be really good for her."

"She's probably not welcome in the pool," Stan said, coming up behind them. "She does have access to the creek down there on the property, and, as soon as we take her, the first thing she does is jump into the middle of the water."

"I don't blame her," Finn said. "On a hot day …"

Helga laid here, panting in the heat, as Fiona gently rubbed her ribs. Stan looked down at the coffee and the cinnamon bun and said, "You guys will ruin your dinner."

"We were just thinking that," Finn said, taking a bite anyway. "I told Dennis that we probably didn't need anything, but he suggested we have this now and then dinner at six."

"You guys do that," Stan said, laughing. "I'm heading up to get real food."

"It's early yet, isn't it?" Fiona asked.

"It is," Stan said, "but I figured, if I could get my dinner now, I could go back down to the puppies."

"How's the mom doing?" Finn asked, hating that he'd forgotten about her.

"She's pulled through," he said, "and she's doing just fine. The babies are with her all the time, and she has milk."

Finn looked over at Fiona. "Do you want to get dressed and get food, or are you content?"

She grabbed his hand, lacing her fingers with his, and whispered, "I'm very content." Then she stretched out again, Helga still laying across her middle.

He had to admit he hadn't had a day like this in months and months. As he looked back on his years of naval service, and then the accident as a defining moment in his world, and all the surgeries and recuperation and hell since then, like her, he realized that this was a special moment.

Chapter 12

LYING HERE UNDER the afternoon sun, resting beside the pool with Finn by her side and Helga across her lap ... was utterly perfect. She didn't want to move. Just to hear that the lawsuit had been dropped was magic to her ears and, indeed, lifted a huge weight off her shoulders. She hadn't even realized how much of a weight it had become. It hadn't been there for long but long enough to destroy her good mood. She was so grateful that the lawsuit wasn't going ahead and that the patient could move on. It let her move on too.

She didn't see Finn in the same light. Finn was independent, strong mentally, very capable and emotionally balanced. The fact that he was out here at the pool, even with his colostomy bag on display, was a massive shift. He was stretched out beside her, patting Helga, enjoying the sun. It was also good for his body.

He whispered, "Don't fall asleep like this, or you'll likely burn."

"I know," she murmured, "but it's so damn nice."

"Good for the stress relief, isn't it?"

"Swimming has always been like that for me," she said. "Floating in the water, I feel everything drain away. It's absolutely the best feeling."

"Agreed," he said with a heavy sigh and stretched out.

Long moments later, a breeze came up. "We need to get changed soon."

"Soon, but not yet."

She chuckled in complete agreement. "Any word on the prosthetic?"

"Two days," he said. "It's coming in two days."

"Perfect," she said, "and, if you don't wear it too long right off the bat, to avoid soring up the stump at all, you should be good to go."

He chuckled. "Yes, *Doctor*."

She flushed. "I didn't mean it that way."

He squeezed her fingers. "And I didn't take it that way. It's what I did last time, so I'm certainly aware that that was a big mistake to avoid this time."

"Good," she said. "I know that you'll find your mobility so much more improved when you have it back again."

"I've become accustomed to the wheelchair," he said. "The crutches still sore up my back sometimes, but that's been coming along a lot better too."

"How is the structural-integrity work going?"

"Amazingly well," he said with surprise. "My shoulders are moving back into the proper posture. I'm holding my head straighter over my spine instead of pushed forward. Shane wants me to get my prosthetic too because having that balance will help me to keep my hips properly positioned over my heels, and everything else will fall into place much easier."

"The human body is a marvel," she whispered, feeling sleep trying to drag her under. "Are you tired right now?"

"Tired but not sleepy."

"If I drift off for a few minutes, can you make sure it's just a few minutes?"

"Sure," he said. "How about ten tops?"

She smiled and let her stress drop down yet another notch. She didn't really fall asleep; she just lay here in her deep state, letting everything wash over her. "Have you seen Lovely lately?" she murmured sleepily.

He chuckled. "I thought you were supposed to be sleeping."

"I'm just drifting. But Lovely is adorable."

"I haven't seen her for a few days now," he said, "or the puppies."

"If they're back with Mom, they'll be good for a while," she said. "Once they start walking and waddling around, they're beyond adorable."

"Right." He said, "I love animals of all kinds." He straightened and looked up toward the deck on the main floor. "I think I hear a louder crowd up top." He smiled and said, "I gather that means it's dinnertime."

Fiona opened her eyes more and said, "It sounds like it."

Then Helga's head popped up. She stood the rest of the way up, stepping on Fiona's stomach, and then the huge dog clambered up the stairway to join everyone gathering in the dining area.

Fiona and Finn laughed at her antics to get more loving and to get more food.

Fiona sighed. "We want to wait for the rush to go by anyway."

"Absolutely." He sat up slowly and said, "Not to mention the fact that it'll take me a bit of time to get back to my room and to get changed."

"Right, me too," she said. She glanced over at him. "Meet back up there in what, thirty minutes?"

He looked at his wheelchair, considered the time frame

and said, "Make it forty, maybe forty-five," he said, "and I'll have a shower too."

"Done," she said. She watched as he hopped along the edge of the pool to his wheelchair and made his way into the seat. When he released the brake and turned himself around, she slid back into the water and did another ten laps. Feeling better and a little more tired, she pulled out at the shallow end and grabbed her towel. She wrapped it around her and headed for her own place.

There, she quickly had a shower and decided to wear one of her flowing dresses again. There was just something so very feminine about wearing these. They felt good for her soul. Dressed again, she quickly rebraided her hair and walked up early, hoping to meet him at his room.

He was just coming out as she walked down the hallway. He looked up at her and smiled. "Fancy meeting you here."

She glanced in at his room and his sketchbooks on the bed. "Do you want to stay and sketch?" she asked.

"No," he said. "I'll come back and sketch again later."

He closed the door firmly, and the two of them headed down for dinner. As soon as they entered the dining room, several people called to them. She looked over and said, "Where do you want to sit?"

"Actually, I wouldn't mind spending time with Elliot. Are you up for that?"

She smiled, delighted to be invited. "Absolutely. Let's get food first."

Finn shouted back at Elliot, then directed them toward the food. "Unless you want to go someplace with your other friends," he said.

"No," she said, "I'm happy to be with you and yours."

IT ALMOST FELT like a date again but more comfortable and cozier. Special maybe. In a way, something was so natural about being with Fiona that Finn knew it probably was obvious to everybody around them—and he didn't care one bit. When he approached to see Dennis standing behind the counter again, Finn grinned. "So what's on tap tonight?"

Dennis reeled off the huge menu, leaving Finn wondering what to choose. But he watched as Fiona picked up several pieces of fried chicken and coleslaw. "Oh, man," he said, "I haven't had good fried chicken in forever."

"My favorite recipe," Dennis said, leaning forward. "And it's really mine and my grandmother's."

"That's an easy choice then," Finn said, holding out his plate.

Dennis took four pieces and then grabbed biscuits and filled the rest of his plate with coleslaw.

"You can fill my plate like this anytime," Finn said, grinning widely. He kept on going but didn't really need any of the other food—and there were plenty more choices. They always had lots of food here. He didn't know whether the staff in the back of the counter got to come in and eat as they wanted to afterward or what the deal was, but Finn was delighted. Finally, with everything collected, they rolled over toward where Elliot sat. He had saved them one space but not two. Finn glanced at him. "Can we get an extra seat?"

Elliot immediately stood, grabbed another table and tucked it up to the side. "There is now," he said. "The day I don't find a space for a pretty lady to join us," he said, "is the day I'm dead."

Fiona laughed and placed her tray down. "You always

did have a sweet-talking way with words."

"Hey, I'm not so bad," he said.

"Or so good," she said, waggling her eyebrows.

At that, the table burst out laughing. He loved the way that Fiona settled in nicely with anybody. She wasn't stuck up; she didn't care who was there, and, as long as people were friendly and nice, she was happy to be a part of it. It said a lot about who she was and what she was after in life. And what she'd been through.

Elliot took one look at Finn's plate and said, "Wow, man, can you eat all that?"

"I'll eat all this and go for seconds," Finn promised. "You know me and fried chicken. It's soul food. Nothing like it." He listened to the conversation, but his focus was on his food, and, at his first bite, he almost moaned in delight. When he opened his eyes, Dennis stood off to the side, pointing at him. He lifted his thumb and forefinger in a circle to say, *Awesome*, and then he resumed eating. When he was done with his plate, he settled back to relax. He really wanted more chicken, except he was pretty full.

Just then Dennis appeared by his side with a platter in front of him. "Take a piece or two," he said, handing him the tongs. "You can't be done yet."

There was a perfect drumstick right in front, so he snagged that and then a wing. And then he held up his hand to say no more and added, "But you can put a half-dozen pieces away for me for later, at least for lunch tomorrow."

"Done," Dennis said. "Anytime you want food saved for you, we handle it." He looked over at Fiona and asked, "What about you? Should we pack up a picnic for two?"

"That's not a bad idea," she said in surprise.

"Isn't it your day off tomorrow?" Finn asked.

"It is," she said, "but I'm not going to town. I'm staying around here, so, if you want, we can take lunch out to the horses and see Lovely again."

"You know something?" he said with a gentle smile. "That would be lovely."

At that, everybody else teased the two of them, while Elliot gave Finn a knowing look. But Dennis, with a big smile of satisfaction, disappeared. Finn had to wonder if Dennis hadn't set that up on purpose. Finn leaned over to Fiona and said, "I think Dennis is a bit of a matchmaker."

"Actually, he's a big matchmaker," she said, chuckling. "But it comes from the heart."

She kept working on her plate. It had been half the size of his, and he'd scarfed his so fast that she was still working on her first plate. He finished his last two pieces of chicken and pushed himself slightly back from the table. "That was fantastic."

Elliot grinned at him. "Aren't you glad I told you to get your ass over here?"

Finn nodded. "Absolutely. Should have listened to Dani from the first."

"You should have," Elliot said. "The minute you knew this place was up and running, and you had a way to get in, you should have been here."

"I was still recovering from my last surgery," Finn said. "At least, that's my excuse, and I'm sticking to it."

Elliot reached out and gave him a light smack on the shoulder. "Damn, it's nice to have you here."

"I hear you," he said. "What about the other friends you made?"

"They've gone home," Elliot said. "Although home is not very far away. They're settling in Houston, and we'll stay in touch, probably go into business together. I got about another month here, and then I'll be good to go too."

"That is awesome," Finn exclaimed. "Time just flew by. I hadn't even realized."

"Yep, that's time here," Elliot said, "and I'm almost done. My team thought I was doing pretty well but then not quite so well."

"Well, you're probably better off to stay as long as you need," Finn said. "At least until you're a hundred percent. It's a big, bad world out there and very unforgiving."

It wasn't long before Elliot and his friends at the table got up and left. When they said their goodbyes, Elliot winked at Finn and said, "Time for you two to sit on the deck over on the far side there," he said, "a perfect spot for a couple. Take a coffee, maybe something a little bit stronger, and enjoy." And he disappeared.

Finn looked over at Fiona. "Something a little stronger?"

She laughed. "You're not cleared for alcohol. Every once in a while, a bottle of bubbly comes out, if somebody's got something major to celebrate. But not very often. Aaron and Dani's engagement celebration, yes. As a regular occasion, no."

"So what's this spot for two?" he asked. "Do you know what they're talking about?"

She nodded. "I do, indeed."

Instant jealousy ripped through him.

She looked at him in surprise. "No, not from personal experience."

He chuckled. "Sorry, that was such an instinctive reaction because I hate to think of you with anybody else."

She smiled and said, "Ditto."

And that's just the way life was between them. As far as he was concerned, that made it perfect.

Chapter 13

AFTER DINNER, FIONA went back to the office to check in on something that she'd forgotten about during the day. She said goodbye to Finn as he headed to his room. As she got to the office, Anna sat there, frowning at folders. "Did I mess up?" she asked lightly.

Anna shook her head. "Not really," she said, "just Finn's folder is missing a bunch of information."

"Then it wasn't me," Fiona said. "I have deliberately kept my hands off that just because of our developing relationship."

Anna chuckled. "I can see why," she said. "That former patient really messed you up, didn't he?"

"I just have to be sure that whatever is going on between Finn and me is real," she said, "so I don't want to even know all the details about his condition."

"Well, his condition is fine, just a bunch of stuff hasn't been printed off properly, and some of these consent forms weren't signed."

"Like what?"

"Like the pool, for one," she said.

Immediately Fiona held out her hand. "Give it to me. Plus anything else. I'll take it to him right now. I just left him at his room as it is."

"Hang on a sec. Let me grab it." She quickly printed off

the three forms that she needed, handed her a clipboard and said, "If you can bring them back to me tonight, that'd be great."

Fiona smiled and nodded and immediately headed back to Finn's room. The door wasn't quite closed. She knocked lightly and pushed it open. "Finn, you here?"

The bed was empty. Sketchbooks were on it; he called from the bathroom. "I'm in here," he said. "I'll be a little bit."

"Not a problem," she said. "I have some consent forms for you to sign."

"Leave them on the bed," he said. "I'll sign them when I get back out."

Figuring he was probably getting ready for a shower, she dropped them on the bed and then noticed the sketchbook was open. She looked down and caught sight of the same woman as before, only this time it was complete. She lifted the sketchbook and stared in both shock and admiration. Moments later she recognized the woman. She froze.

It was her.

Tears filled her eyes. The picture was stunning and made her much more beautiful than she was, but, with a few strokes, he'd caught her nose, her eyes, the look on her face. It was magical. She sank to the bed, stunned to see the talent, that raw skill on the page in front of her like that.

How could he not go pro?

This was beyond belief. She quickly flipped through the pages and realized that every damn page of the sketchbook was filled with pictures of her.

Various stages.

Various poses.

Various looks.

She shook her head in shock, and in the back of her mind came that same ugly suspicion again. She didn't quite know what to do. Over forty drawings of her were here, and yet, she hadn't counted, but the book only held forty-five sheets, and hardly any were blank. Her breath shuddered in her chest at the horrified realization that he was quite likely way too fixated on her, just as Ziegler had been. When she heard him in the bathroom, washing his hands, she quickly dropped the sketchbook and disappeared.

She needed time to think about this. Not going back to Anna, Fiona raced outside to the animals. She stood here, propped up against the fence inside the horse pen, Lovely wandering in front of her, as Fiona tried to calm down, but she was afraid it was way too late for that. After what she'd been through with her other patient, she couldn't go through it again. She'd cared about the other patient but on a strictly professional level.

This patient she cared about on a whole different level. The tears, once they started, just wouldn't stop. She couldn't even begin to gain control. When they finally slowed and came to an end, she found herself curled up on the ground, her back against the post, her arms wrapped on her knees, hugging them tightly. As she lifted her head and stared at the much different panorama around her, she whispered, "Oh, dear God."

She didn't know how long she'd been lying there, but her whole world had collapsed in a wave of fear. She lay here for a long moment as she didn't quite know how to deal with this new reality. A few moments after that, she finally shifted and heard a voice behind her.

"It's not what you think."

She stiffened, recognizing Finn's voice. She didn't know

what to say, but she didn't have to say anything. He knew that wasn't an option here. He must have seen her. But then how long had he been here, watching her cry?

"I know you probably don't want to believe me," he said, his voice coming a little bit closer.

She didn't turn around but could hear the crutches as he made several hops and steps and then worked his way slowly toward the fence. "If you'd looked at the other sketchbook," he said, "you would have seen that it's filled with pictures of Dani."

She stiffened at that and frowned. *Dani?*

"I started doing it for her, thinking that maybe it would be a nice gift for her wedding, if I could capture just the right look. She's done so much for this place, I wanted to have something to give back." His voice was sad, almost apologetic.

Fiona twisted slightly to look and saw him only a few feet from her on the other side of the railings.

"And, while I was drawing some of her, I also started to draw some of you," he said. "There's something very special about your face, the way it caught my pencil, or my pencil caught you," he said. "And I just couldn't stop drawing. Dani hasn't seen the ones of her, but she has seen a couple that I've done of you."

At that, Fiona didn't know what to say. "You know what it looks like, don't you?"

"I know what it looks like to you," he said slowly. "But I don't think it would look that way to anybody else."

"How can it not?" she asked. "I mean, how could I possibly not make the same comparison? The lawsuit itself was just dropped after Dani's lawyers had a talk with Zeigler's legal team. But it was traumatic at the time of our initial confrontation. Then I forgot about it until the whole mess reared up again as a lawsuit. I don't want to be put in that position again."

"I'm not fixated on you," he said, his voice steady. "I'm not making you into somebody who you aren't."

She gave a broken laugh. "And yet, our positions are so very different that I don't know that you understand just how you feel," she said.

"I understand exactly how I feel." This time his voice was stronger. Adamant. And a little bit angry.

Well, she understood that feeling. She hopped to her feet, turned and glared at him. "Don't you understand what this looks like?"

He stared at her in astonishment. "Those photos should tell you more than anything how I feel about you," he said bluntly. "Words don't have anywhere near the same impact as something like that, something that I created from my heart."

At that, she took a step back. Confused, she shoved her hands in her pockets. "I want to believe that's how you see me," she said, "but how am I supposed to separate the patient-nurse relationship?"

"You don't get it, do you?" he asked, tilting his head ever-so-slightly to the side. "Just because the other guy was crazy and co-dependent and needed to know that you were there as that shining beacon in order to make the kind of progress he did, he didn't know how to disassociate from it and to keep it within reality," he said. "I highly doubt you went out and had dinners with him or that you sat out in the fields and had coffee with him, did you?"

"No," she shook her head. "Of course not."

"Of course not," he repeated. "Because that wasn't the

relationship you had with him. The relationship he had with you was in his mind. You had a professional relationship with him. That's all there was, and that's why, when you found out how he felt, it was such a shock. You and I have already been dancing around this for weeks. The fact that I drew those pictures has nothing to do with an obsessed mind or somebody who doesn't know the reality of this relationship," he said quietly. "It's entirely pictures of a man who can't get you out of his mind but for all the right reasons."

She looked at him hesitantly.

He nodded. "I get that that's your past, and it's some of your garbage that you have to toss away, but this is your opportunity to do so. You can't judge what we have by the same brush of the relationship he had in his mind. That wasn't real. What we have is real."

She could feel the tears coming into her eyes again. She wiped them away impatiently.

"The thing is, you have to look at how you feel yourself. Maybe this is something that I'm making up," he said, suddenly backtracking. "Maybe I'm the one who made the mistake here. Maybe you don't care about me." He turned away slightly, looking at the horizon. "Maybe you're right. Maybe I'm the one out to lunch here. In which case I need to pull back in a big way. I was planning a future. I was planning on living together, marriage, the whole nine yards," he said, "but I don't want to be thought of the same way as this Ziegler guy and looked upon the way everybody else here looks upon him. If I'm totally out to lunch," he said, his voice harsh, "then you need to tell me. And I'll stop this now."

Slowly he made his way back to the rehab center.

"It's not," she said.

He froze and shifted slightly so he could look at her. "It's not what?"

She took a deep breath. "It's not like that."

"I need more than that," he said, his face stiff and his shoulders rigid. "I get that you've got a problem with us having a relationship. I get that you're afraid that I don't know what my own mind is. And that, in a way, is very insulting because I do know my own mind. I didn't come here looking for an angel. I didn't come here for any other reason than hoping to heal. I've come further and farther and better than I had even thought possible since arriving here, but one of my greatest joys was also meeting you. I am not in any danger of confusing the two. Are you?"

She walked toward him, feeling a shakiness inside, a sense that she was on the brink of losing something that she would regret forever. "No," she said. "I saw those drawings, and it just brought up all the fear and pain and nightmares I've had for the last few weeks. I didn't compare the two of you. You two are so different. In fact, I went out of my way to avoid doing that, but seeing those sketches …"

"I get that," he said steadily, his gaze never leaving hers.

She liked that about him. He was always very much a person who stared down trouble. He looked it in the eye and dared it to take over his life. He was the kind to deal with stuff and to not shove it under the rug.

She wasn't so sure that she was.

This conversation was hard. She would have to open herself up even more. She'd spent a lot of time these last few years building up those walls—first due to her cheating boyfriend and later due to her deluded patient—and now she would have to break both those walls down.

"What I feel is real," she said with a heavy sigh. "The

sketches just pushed a button, and all that grief, pain and confusion came out. There's so much fear." She stopped, closed her eyes for a moment and said, "Not about you or about how I feel about you. But that you didn't feel that way about me. That I was making a mistake all over again. That I had inadvertently hurt somebody else, in this case, somebody I cared about very much."

"You need to understand how I feel," he said. "I've tried to make it obvious. I've tried to make this easy. But there's nothing ever easy about relationships. Dani knows how I feel about you. She's also warned me to be careful."

At that, Fiona chuckled. "Yeah, that's Dani. Besides, she wants the world to be happy."

"I'm totally okay with the world being happy too," he said. "In a way, I'd prefer it because it's much easier on all of us. And it's nice, when you're happy, to want everybody around you to be happy. But life isn't always that way. So we're either moving forward, and you're letting this go completely and forever, and you'll never doubt how I feel again," he said, with a note of warning, "or we have to decide that this is not built on reality and not built on trust … because, without trust, there's nothing."

She felt his words almost like arrows to her heart, but she also heard the truth behind them.

"I hear. I understand," she said, "and I do trust you, and I do want to move forward. But you also need to understand that sometimes little things can set off hidden emotions. So, as much as I may never want to be afraid or to not trust you again or to want this to ever rear its ugly head again, I *can't* promise that. I will do my best to deal with it when it comes up, and I will certainly want to talk to you about it then," she said, "but don't ask something of me that is not possible to give."

He looked at her, and a slow smile dawned.

She finally realized he stood here, a crutch under one arm, but his arms were open. She closed the gap between them in seconds. As his arms tightened around her, she burrowed in close, and he whispered, "Good answer. None of us are perfect. None of us can guarantee how we'll react in a given situation. I'm willing to try. And that's all I ask of you."

She squeezed him tight. "Trying is easy," she said. "But doing a really good job at it, that's not quite so easy."

He chuckled. "But you're doing so well at everything else," he said, "I'm sure you'll do fine at this." He kissed her gently on her temple and then her nose. "Feeling better?"

She nodded slightly and tucked her head closer into his neck. "I do have to ask you something though," she whispered. She could feel him stiffen beneath her. She gave him a gentle squeeze and then pulled back. "Do I really look like that to you?"

He winked and said, "Honestly, you look way better. If I thought I could get my fingers to draw you the way I see you, it would be perfect. I keep trying. But you're so very precious," he whispered, "and so very beautiful."

She smiled up at him. "Is that because it was drawn by somebody who—"

He placed a finger against her lips, stopping her words. He leaned forward, and he whispered, "If you're asking, the answer is yes," he said. "I do love you."

Her smile, when it came, blossomed across her face, and her breath caught in her throat. She threw her arms around his neck and whispered, "Well, thank heavens for that."

He chuckled, grasped her chin gently with his fingers

and lowered his head and stared into her eyes. "Now, shall we take a moment and be us and enjoy the journey?"

She nodded. "Yes, please."

And he lowered his head, and he kissed her. Not just for today, not just for tomorrow, but a kiss of love for all the tomorrows flowing forward.

And she'd never ever been happier.

Epilogue

G REGORY PARKINS STARED at the application in his hand and wondered. He'd had this thing printed off and filled out half a dozen times in the last couple weeks, and every time he had balled it up and threw it away. Hathaway House was just one of many other rehab centers that he had thought of going to. He knew he needed to go to this one though, but it wasn't so much for himself but because of the woman he had left behind.

He wouldn't have had a clue that she was even there if not for a write-up about Hathaway House that had hit the internet and gone viral. Something about Dani and her father and what they had accomplished since they built the center. The article had piqued his interest, and he'd gone looking to see what kind of a rehab center it was. His research had led him to photographs of the staff at the center, and there, sure enough, he'd seen the photo that had sent him into a tailspin.

Meredith, the woman he had left behind the last time he had headed off on a mission. It had already been five years, but he'd never forgotten her. Gregory could only hope that she'd never forgotten him either. But the chances were, she'd moved on, was likely married and had a family by now.

But he didn't know that. Should he reach out to her or just ignore this? *Ignore?* His laugh was hollow, completely devoid of emotions. He knew he couldn't ignore her. Wasn't that evident by the number of times he'd filled out the paper applications only to crumple them up and throw them away? He and Meredith had spent three wonderful weeks together, and he thought he'd found *the one*.

When he had finally told her that he was leaving again, she'd been heartbroken. Desolate. Her brother had died overseas, and she didn't want to deal with the same kind of loss again. Gregory understood, but he'd signed up for the navy as soon as he could, right out of school. He'd been honored to join, and his career had fulfilled him every year since. No way would he walk away at that point.

As soon as he left her, he regretted his decision.

He knew he should have turned around and found a way to make this work, but instead, he'd buried himself in his work and had tried to forget her. And, for a time, he'd managed. But then he had been blown up by an IED. Now, if he went to look for her, he would feel like *he* was second-best, like he had only come back to her because he was no longer whole. No longer fit for the navy, so she was his second choice.

Again. Just like before. But for different reasons.

He didn't want that. Nor did he want her to feel that way.

Yet, if she was still at the rehab center and single, they had a chance to work on a whole new level of a relationship. And with so many more problems than they had originally. Even to him, that sounded harsh, but the truth was often harsh. He didn't even know why she would want him back in this state. He'd be offering her less than what he had been before, and yet, he'd walked away from her.

He snorted.

As if he were fully capable of walking away anymore. Because he no longer could. ... Not without crutches, a wheelchair or a prosthetic.

Gregory laid the paperwork off to the side. He had also filled out the online form but hadn't really worked on the last couple questions, determined to at least do that much, as he knew Hathaway House could help him physically if nothing else. Maybe he could walk away from her again and not regret it this time. Maybe, just maybe, he could find a whole new life. Sometimes one had to go through the pain to get to the closure, and eventually, to reach a new life at the other end.

He quickly filled out the last few questions online; then his gaze landed on Meredith's picture once more. Not giving himself much chance to rethink anything, he reviewed the online application—the same as the physical paperwork he had filled out a dozen times—and hit Send.

For better or for worse, his application was in.

This concludes Book 6 of Hathaway House: Finn.
Read about Gregory: Hathaway House, Book 7

Hathaway House: Gregory (Book #7)

Welcome to Hathaway House, a heartwarming military romance series from USA TODAY best-selling author Dale Mayer. Here you'll meet a whole new group of friends, along with a few favorite characters from Heroes for Hire. Instead of action, you'll find emotion. Instead of suspense, you'll find healing. Instead of romance, ... oh, wait. ... There is romance—of course!"

Welcome to Hathaway House. Rehab Center. Safe Haven. Second chance at life and love.

Navy SEAL Gregory Parkins knows he's not so bad off as to need what Hathaway House offers, but he'll do anything to get in. RN Meredith Anderson is there, and Greg loves Meredith. In the time since they split up, his life has been one disaster after another, including the one that ended his career—the career that separated them in the first place.

Meredith was horrified to hear what happened to Gregory. But seeing his file was an even bigger shock. Greg thinks he's basically back to normal, but Meredith knows he has a long way to go. She doesn't know how to tell him, without running the risk of him leaving Hathaway House before his healing can really take place.

But the last thing she wants is for him to walk away from her again. Not if there is any chance that they can find their way back to each other ...

Book 7 is available now!

To find out more visit Dale Mayer's website.

http://smarturl.it/DMGregoryUniversal

Author's Note

Thank you for reading Finn: Hathaway House, Book 6! If you enjoyed the book, please take a moment and leave a short review.

Dear reader,

I love to hear from readers, and you can contact me at my website: www.dalemayer.com or at my Facebook author page. To be informed of new releases and special offers, sign up for my newsletter or follow me on BookBub. And if you are interested in joining Dale Mayer's Reader Group, here is the Facebook sign up page.
facebook.com/groups/402384989872660

Cheers,
Dale Mayer

Get THREE Free Books Now!

Have you met the SEALS of Honor?

SEALs of Honor Books 1, 2, and 3. Follow the stories of brave, badass warriors who serve their country with honor and love their women to the limits of life and death.

Read Mason, Hawk, and Dane right now for FREE.

Go here and tell me where to send them!
http://smarturl.it/EthanBofB

About the Author

Dale Mayer is a USA Today bestselling author best known for her Psychic Visions and Family Blood Ties series. Her contemporary romances are raw and full of passion and emotion (Second Chances, SKIN), her thrillers will keep you guessing (By Death series), and her romantic comedies will keep you giggling (It's a Dog's Life and Charmin Marvin Romantic Comedy series).

She honors the stories that come to her – and some of them are crazy and break all the rules and cross multiple genres!

To go with her fiction, she also writes nonfiction in many different fields with books available on resume writing, companion gardening and the US mortgage system. She has recently published her Career Essentials Series. All her books are available in print and ebook format.

Connect with Dale Mayer Online

Dale's Website – www.dalemayer.com
Twitter – @DaleMayer
Facebook – dalemayer.com/fb
BookBub – bookbub.com/authors/dale-mayer

Also by Dale Mayer

Published Adult Books:

Hathaway House
Aaron, Book 1
Brock, Book 2
Cole, Book 3
Denton, Book 4
Elliot, Book 5
Finn, Book 6
Gregory, Book 7

The K9 Files
Ethan, Book 1
Pierce, Book 2
Zane, Book 3
Blaze, Book 4
Lucas, Book 5
Parker, Book 6
Carter, Book 7

Lovely Lethal Gardens
Arsenic in the Azaleas, Book 1
Bones in the Begonias, Book 2
Corpse in the Carnations, Book 3
Daggers in the Dahlias, Book 4
Evidence in the Echinacea, Book 5
Footprints in the Ferns, Book 6

Gun in the Gardenias, Book 7
Handcuffs in the Heather, Book 8

Psychic Vision Series
Tuesday's Child
Hide 'n Go Seek
Maddy's Floor
Garden of Sorrow
Knock Knock...
Rare Find
Eyes to the Soul
Now You See Her
Shattered
Into the Abyss
Seeds of Malice
Eye of the Falcon
Itsy-Bitsy Spider
Unmasked
Deep Beneath
From the Ashes
Psychic Visions Books 1–3
Psychic Visions Books 4–6
Psychic Visions Books 7–9

By Death Series
Touched by Death
Haunted by Death
Chilled by Death
By Death Books 1–3

Broken Protocols – Romantic Comedy Series
Cat's Meow
Cat's Pajamas

Cat's Cradle
Cat's Claus
Broken Protocols 1-4

Broken and... Mending
Skin
Scars
Scales (of Justice)
Broken but... Mending 1-3

Glory
Genesis
Tori
Celeste
Glory Trilogy

Biker Blues
Morgan: Biker Blues, Volume 1
Cash: Biker Blues, Volume 2

SEALs of Honor
Mason: SEALs of Honor, Book 1
Hawk: SEALs of Honor, Book 2
Dane: SEALs of Honor, Book 3
Swede: SEALs of Honor, Book 4
Shadow: SEALs of Honor, Book 5
Cooper: SEALs of Honor, Book 6
Markus: SEALs of Honor, Book 7
Evan: SEALs of Honor, Book 8
Mason's Wish: SEALs of Honor, Book 9
Chase: SEALs of Honor, Book 10
Brett: SEALs of Honor, Book 11
Devlin: SEALs of Honor, Book 12

Easton: SEALs of Honor, Book 13
Ryder: SEALs of Honor, Book 14
Macklin: SEALs of Honor, Book 15
Corey: SEALs of Honor, Book 16
Warrick: SEALs of Honor, Book 17
Tanner: SEALs of Honor, Book 18
Jackson: SEALs of Honor, Book 19
Kanen: SEALs of Honor, Book 20
Nelson: SEALs of Honor, Book 21
Taylor: SEALs of Honor, Book 22
SEALs of Honor, Books 1–3
SEALs of Honor, Books 4–6
SEALs of Honor, Books 7–10
SEALs of Honor, Books 11–13
SEALs of Honor, Books 14–16
SEALs of Honor, Books 17–19

Heroes for Hire
Levi's Legend: Heroes for Hire, Book 1
Stone's Surrender: Heroes for Hire, Book 2
Merk's Mistake: Heroes for Hire, Book 3
Rhodes's Reward: Heroes for Hire, Book 4
Flynn's Firecracker: Heroes for Hire, Book 5
Logan's Light: Heroes for Hire, Book 6
Harrison's Heart: Heroes for Hire, Book 7
Saul's Sweetheart: Heroes for Hire, Book 8
Dakota's Delight: Heroes for Hire, Book 9
Michael's Mercy (Part of Sleeper SEAL Series)
Tyson's Treasure: Heroes for Hire, Book 10
Jace's Jewel: Heroes for Hire, Book 11
Rory's Rose: Heroes for Hire, Book 12
Brandon's Bliss: Heroes for Hire, Book 13

Liam's Lily: Heroes for Hire, Book 14
North's Nikki: Heroes for Hire, Book 15
Anders's Angel: Heroes for Hire, Book 16
Reyes's Raina: Heroes for Hire, Book 17
Dezi's Diamond: Heroes for Hire, Book 18
Vince's Vixen: Heroes for Hire, Book 19
Ice's Icing: Heroes for Hire, Book 20
Heroes for Hire, Books 1–3
Heroes for Hire, Books 4–6
Heroes for Hire, Books 7–9
Heroes for Hire, Books 10–12
Heroes for Hire, Books 13–15

SEALs of Steel
Badger: SEALs of Steel, Book 1
Erick: SEALs of Steel, Book 2
Cade: SEALs of Steel, Book 3
Talon: SEALs of Steel, Book 4
Laszlo: SEALs of Steel, Book 5
Geir: SEALs of Steel, Book 6
Jager: SEALs of Steel, Book 7
The Final Reveal: SEALs of Steel, Book 8
SEALs of Steel, Books 1–4
SEALs of Steel, Books 5–8
SEALs of Steel, Books 1–8

Collections
Dare to Be You...
Dare to Love...
Dare to be Strong...
RomanceX3

Standalone Novellas
It's a Dog's Life
Riana's Revenge
Second Chances

Published Young Adult Books:

Family Blood Ties Series
Vampire in Denial
Vampire in Distress
Vampire in Design
Vampire in Deceit
Vampire in Defiance
Vampire in Conflict
Vampire in Chaos
Vampire in Crisis
Vampire in Control
Vampire in Charge
Family Blood Ties Set 1–3
Family Blood Ties Set 1–5
Family Blood Ties Set 4–6
Family Blood Ties Set 7–9
Sian's Solution, A Family Blood Ties Series Prequel
    Novelette

Design series
Dangerous Designs
Deadly Designs
Darkest Designs
Design Series Trilogy

Standalone
In Cassie's Corner

Gem Stone (a Gemma Stone Mystery)
Time Thieves

Published Non-Fiction Books:

Career Essentials
Career Essentials: The Résumé
Career Essentials: The Cover Letter
Career Essentials: The Interview
Career Essentials: 3 in 1

Printed in Great Britain
by Amazon

58618393R10108